between dances

WITHDRAWN

between dances

a novel

Erasmo Guerra

Painted Leaf Press
New York City

Printed in Canada

Cover design by Travis Ward
Typesetting by Brian Brunius

Library of Congress Cataloging-in-Publication Data

Guerra, Erasmo.
   Between dances : a novel / by Erasmo Guerra.
      p. cm.
   ISBN 1-891305-23-9
      1. Young men--New York (State)--New York--Fiction.
      2. Gay men--New York (State)--New York--Fiction.
      3. New York (N.Y.)--Fiction.
      I. Title.

PS3557.U338 B4 2000
813'.54--dc21

99-087729

Conventional wisdom is death to our souls

Live where you fear to live

Destroy your reputations

Be notorious

~Rumi~

fall

one

Marco did not want to dance. He did not want to get back onstage and do his last number for the night. The hour had dragged its naked ass to three in the morning and everything hurt and ached. The scrap between his legs felt raw from pulling on it too many times and from having too many strange men suck it in his hotel room between dances. It hurt to even touch it.

He stood behind the back curtain, listening to his song and its forced cheer collapsing like soap bubbles. What was he doing here, he wondered. The question inevitably asked itself at some point during the night, the interrogative words loud and demanding as the songs that blared over the speakers. He lanced those suspended moments with whatever excuses he found or let them fall and shatter from their own weight. They always did. If he ignored them long enough. Tonight, with his exhaustion weighing him down, he thought it better to be done with it, to part the curtains and go out before the DJ decided to start the record again. He pushed himself out onstage and stripped to his white briefs without choreographing any of his moves to the music. He then slipped behind the curtain again, to the narrow corridor backstage. The gay dancers, the ones who admitted it, stroked off here. The straight ones jerked off on the other side, in the main room with the lockers. In whatever part of the theater he stood, however, the same dingy smell of sweaty crotches and damp bills penetrated his senses.

He had little more than a minute now. A minute to get himself hard and back out for his second song. This was the "spectacular" part of the live show to which the ads in the papers referred: an uncompromising look at his body. The audience expected him hard, but already he could hear its hiss of disappointment once he went back out there. He didn't care though. He only wanted to get back to his room to sleep.

Marco moved to the end of the corridor and pulled off his underwear. He made sure his money was still in his sock and then laced his boots back on slowly, steadying his breath, searching for a fragmentary thought or image that could get him off. He sat on his clothes over the radiator and stroked himself to the memory of a guy in a pool. The guy had been in a porn magazine Marco had bought last week, but the magazine was in his locker, and he didn't have enough time to go dig it out. Besides, he didn't want to deal with the guys in the other room.

He heard their voices, pinched and shallow, as if tightly holding their breath. They were arguing about the female strippers they had picked up after last night's show and, most like it, were passing around a smoldering joint. His concentration splintered and broke so that in his mind there floated the disembodied parts of the tanned guy, the aquamarine water, the long white pool chair. The john Marco had been with earlier that night suddenly swam into his head. That guy was as worn as a seat in the theater, stained and banged up and suspiciously mute. Looking at him, even by the warm lights of the bedside lamps, had made Marco want to leave the business and perhaps the city. Thinking about the guy in the pool had helped then. He wasn't much help now.

Marco tried to call in the other guys from the magazine, the way he sometimes did when he had the magazine with him, turning the pages quickly, holding each picture for a moment, all of them building to an eventual rush of blood. When that didn't work, he simply prayed, making a *promesa* to *San Juditas*, the way his mother taught him. *San Juditas* was the patron saint of lost causes, but this particular night, even he was of no use.

Marco pulled at himself, slapping the dead skin against his hips, forcing blood to it, but it remained limp. Patrick appeared at the other end of the corridor, by the edge of the steps. He stood there, naked, pulling on his own soft flesh.

"Sorry," he said. "Didn't know you were here."

"That's all right," Marco offered. "This thing ain't getting up anyway. I think I killed it."

"Forget it. It's the last dance. There ain't nobody out there."

Patrick came down and stood off to the side, stroking himself without apology. His eyebrows butted into a single thick line. The rest of his face, though handsome, looked hammered by a stony seriousness. All the dancers had that aggravated look when they needed to get hard.

"Here," Patrick said, spitting into his hands and grabbing Marco's dick.

Marco watched the stairs, afraid one of the other guys would find them. Patrick didn't seem worried. He massaged Marco's bruised flesh, taking it in the palm of his hands and finally his mouth. The second song came up then, Boy George singing a remixed version of "Do You Really Want To Hurt Me." The lyrics were a bit pathetic, but Marco preferred them over the melodramatic love songs that most of the other guys danced to. Those songs never felt honest to him.

The red lights came on full and bled under the back curtain. Marco's cue. He was hard, but he couldn't feel it. His dick seemed to belong to someone else. He kissed Patrick, and feeling nothing at all, his entire body numbed, he rushed out onstage.

No one clapped. The few men that remained for the last show didn't care about Marco's hard-on. They didn't seem to care about anything. They were either too drunk to notice him or had fallen asleep, heads back against their seats, mouths open. Marco danced anyway, as if enjoying himself, though he knew he didn't have to. This was the last dance and he could do more dancing and less showing. He could enjoy himself moving around the stage instead of pretending so the men could get off or think he might be fun to be with in a private show. He swung his arms overhead and rocked his pelvis, his soft thrusts leading him across the stage and up the ramp that plunged into the field of empty seats. He always tried to make a show of it since the muscle guys did nothing more than strike poses as if in a body-building competition, and the others strutted around, winking and pointing at the men in the audience as if in some defunct lounge act.

Marco danced. He had been dancing since before he was even able to dress himself. His mother would button and zip him into his clothes, sometimes forcing him into wearing a cheap clip-on tie. His father would have already eaten his dinner and left the house for whatever place the dance was going to be. He was the lead *chamaco* for the band Los Chamacos del Rio. They played the entire Valley, appeared even once on El Show de Tony Perales. The whole family went to his gigs. Marco and his little brother, *negro*, they called him, enjoyed the late nights, running among the dancing bodies, playing tag or hide-and-seek, licking the beer caps they collected. The adults were either too drunk or set on getting laid or into a fight to care about whatever they did. Even their mother got swept up, dancing with her brothers, one after another, exhausting them and crippling their already bad feet, lamed by their pointy boots. If his mother ever sat out a song, she usually caught Marco and his brother sliding on their knees, across the polished floors of the dance hall. She'd clatter over in her spiked heels and yank them to their feet, cursing them as *hijos de la mañana*, pulling them back to their table where she would make them sit with *las cuatas*, their twin sisters with lip-glossed mouths tight as the ironed curls in their hair. *Las cuatas* only whined about how they would rather be at home watching television or talking on the phone. His mother would ignore their complaints, biting her painted fingernails, pouring

8

herself another vodka grapefruit. She would slug back her disappointment that no one danced with the musicians, not even their wives. Then she would look over at Marco and wink, as if he had suddenly become her little king again, *mi rey,* as she liked to say, and she'd pull him out to the dance floor when the next *corrido* shot out with its shattering *grito.*

Tonight, at the theater, the song didn't go to the end. The DJ stopped it before the second chorus. A weary clap struggled up from the back, but it was too dark for Marco to notice who it was. He hoped it was Chris. He hadn't seen Chris in months.

As the last dancer did his number, Marco went to his locker for his magazine. He needed it for the finale. He didn't think he would get Patrick's help again since he found him in the main room, sitting on one of the benches, listening to the other guys talk about how they were going back to the strip joint. Dallas, one of the muscle guys, leaned up against the lockers and worked his oiled dick with one hand. With the other he held a porn magazine.

"I know you ain't going," he told Marco, then turned to everyone else. "Kid gets his rocks off watching us. We should start charging him."

Weak laughter broke out like the distant rumble of a subway train. Everyone seemed too battered to offer any more. The other dancers were preoccupied with getting themselves ready for the finale or ignored it altogether and lazily picked at the blackheads on their chins or stretched out on the benches with their arms over their eyes. Even Dallas gave up and flung his magazine into his locker. He posed for himself in the mirror. With his distended muscles and burnt-orange skin—the results of too many hours in a gym and tanning booth—he looked like a sideshow freak on the Coney Island boardwalk. All the muscle guys did. Not every john found it attractive. Marco worked the post-adolescent look. Under the colored stage lights, he looked younger than his age. One night, when the female strippers came to the theater to wait for Dallas and the other guys, the women flocked around him in their sequined dresses, tousled his hair and wondered if he was legal enough to dance.

9

The last song spun down and Marco crossed behind the curtain to the other side of the backstage, but even with his magazine and the other naked guys standing by him, he couldn't get hard for the finale. He looked for Patrick, but Patrick must have stayed by the lockers because he wasn't around. Marco thought it might be for the best. He didn't want Patrick to think he was interested in him.

The DJ called everyone back to the stage and Marco went out and stood under the bright lights with a limp dick like everybody else. He thought about those women again, figured they had it easy. They could fake their excitement.

The muscle guys huddled together to the right of the stage, slapping one another on the ass and bending over to fart into what remained of the audience. Marco looked out into the shadowy seats, but the stage lights were on full, blinding with their brilliance. He couldn't make out if anyone in the rear seats was Chris.

Marco dressed quickly and went out to the lounge where a few crumpled old men yanked at the gay hair corkscrewing out of their ears as they waited for the final exit parade of dancers. Marco didn't bother with them. (The stragglers usually didn't have any money, or the money they did have was never enough to buy off his fatigue and need for sleep.) He checked the theater, the box office, and then the DJ booth, but those places were empty and Chris was nowhere. His only surprise came from the sudden need to see him.

He slipped into the bathroom to splash water on his face. He avoided his reflection in the mirror. He had wasted too many years looking at himself in mirrors and in the reflections of glass storefronts and car windshields. He knew what he looked like, and at the end of a dance marathon, he could feel it to his teeth. His eyes would be lined in heavy red strokes, weary from watching too many men watch him. His face would be greasy, slick pores opened wide or clogged with the beginnings of pimples from staying up late. His father had told him that he wouldn't get any more pimples once he started dating girls. Marco figured he meant he wouldn't get any more pimples once he started having sex, but here he was in his early twenties, having more sex than he wanted, and his face still broke out with regularity. He hoped the blemishes made him look young, like a hormonal adolescent, like some of the johns said. He wanted to believe them, pushing out the dream he had been having lately, a dream in which he goes to the theater or bar and waits for the men to come to him, but none do, until finally another hustler begins talking to him as if to make a proposition. Marco tells him he's selling too and the guy combusts into a fireball of laughter. It isn't until he goes to the bathroom that Marco sees how old he is, wrinkled and spotted with an age no dim room could mask.

Standing here in the bathroom with its unsettling blue light, Marco had the vague sense that the particular night of his dreams wasn't too far off. His twenty-fourth birthday was only a few months away. Then what? He didn't know. He only started thinking about what he might do, or where he might go, after tonight's john left him feeling as if he had really worked for every dollar. The money was far from easy now, and soon, he knew, he wouldn't be able to make any. And he had nothing saved. All the money he made was spent on bills or rent or food. The money disappeared faster than a yellow cab hurtling down Broadway.

"Thought you'd already left," Patrick said, coming into the bathroom, his breath heavy and smelling of smoke. "You going out tonight? The Factory should be hot around now."

"I couldn't dance another song." Marco reached for the paper towels to dry his damp face. He couldn't remember the last time he had gone out to a club after a night at the theater. It must have been about the time Chris stopped working, or soon after. He looked at Patrick who said nothing, leaning against the sink, a faint expression of concern darkening his forehead.

"You going back to your room?" Patrick asked.

"No," Marco said, and then lied, "I'm meeting a friend downtown."

He said it only to discourage Patrick from making any proposals. He didn't want to go dancing with him, or back to the hotel room, or to Patrick's apartment as they had the last time. More than anything, Marco wanted to believe that Chris waited for him.

He dried his hands thinking this was the end of it, he would throw the paper towel into the wastebasket and leave the theater altogether, the damp paper putting out whatever embers of interest smoldered in Patrick's crotch. But no, the rejection only seemed to fan them. Patrick asked Marco if he wanted to share a cab. He was headed downtown too. Marco could have said no, but he accepted the offer, thought he might as well go see Chris.

The ride was quiet except for the incessant hollow sound of the vents. They spewed an air so hot it was as if the car was coughing up all the heated air it had swallowed during the summer months.

"You're not going out to Flashdancers with the other guys?" Marco asked Patrick.

"What for?"

"I thought you were into that."

"I'm not. I don't like going there at all. It's pretty sleazy going there to buy those whores. I don't do that. I have a girlfriend."

"Jennifer, right?"

"Jane."

Patrick said her name with a dull smile like he had the night she walked in on them at Patrick's apartment. Marco couldn't remember what she looked like, the anger and surprise that had percolated into his eyes that night had washed out her face.

"I hate cheating on her," Patrick said, his voice serious and apologetic. "She's too much of a good friend, you know. Sometimes I think we're better friends than lovers, but I like her. It's like she knows what I'm thinking and I know what she's thinking. Like soul mates or something."

"She knows you dance?"

"Sure. She's even come by a few times with her friends."

"Nothing about the theater shocks me either, I guess." Marco looked out at the dim impressions of the city, the dark and disinterested streets flipping past like pages in a waiting room magazine. "But I don't think I could ever get involved with anyone who does this for a living." The words came out flat and measured. He had said them so many times. "It's too much to worry about. Like what if they fall in love with somebody, you know?"

"Well, my girlfriend doesn't have to worry about that. I don't really like men all that much." Patrick squeezed Marco's leg as if in consolation.

Marco moved his leg away. "What's all that much?"

"Well, money makes the difference."

"Is this where you tell me how much I owe you for your help back there?"

"Nah. I wanted to do that. It's on the house."

The cab made a sharp turn onto Second Avenue, sliding them closer together. Patrick had a sweet stink to him, like the incense some drivers burned in their cabs. Marco imagined the heated smell unfurling and spiraling around him, dizzying him, making him doubt what he thought he wanted. He had made up his mind that he would never go home with Patrick again or with any straight guy. The experience always left him feeling used like no john did, because at least a john paid money. The straight guys never gave him much of anything other than a momentary thrill, the fleeting thought that he might be their first. He didn't believe that anymore. Chris had convinced him that when a guy at the theater said he was straight, it only meant straight to bed and straight up the ass.

"Where are you going anyway?" Patrick teased, "to see your boyfriend?"

"No, just a friend."

"You don't want to go back to my place? We don't have to do anything, you know, just hang out or whatever."

"What about Jennifer?"

"She's gone to Toronto to visit her folks."

"Wasn't that where she was supposed to be last time?"

Patrick smiled and then opened his mouth to say something, but his lips hung there, his teeth a faint glow from the passing headlights of other cabs rushing through the black streets. He said, "You're not like the other guys, Marco."

His name wasn't Marco, but he used it at the theater and hardly answered to his real name anymore. Patrick wasn't Patrick's real name either. His girlfriend had cried out some other name that Marco didn't remember now.

"Let's go back to my place," Patrick whispered.

"My friend is waiting."

"He's really waiting for you?"

Before he could insist that he was, the cab stopped on East Seventeenth by the gothic wrought-iron fence of Stuyvesant Park. Marco got out. Patrick slipped him a piece of paper on which he had scrawled a phone number and what Marco assumed to be his real name. Marco pulled out a few bills for the cab, but Patrick wouldn't take it.

"Call me and it'll be even," he said. "Besides, I scored more than you tonight."

"Whatever you say." Marco laughed and shut the door.

Patrick put a loose fist to his ear in the shape of a phone. Marco nodded. The cab sped off and Marco headed for the hotel where Chris lived.

Hotel Seventeen could have been any other roach-trap in the city were it not for the fashion photographers who used it as a location for their bohemian-inspired shoots and the small-time celebrity club kids who lived there. The residents were roomed according to the degree of their nocturnal fame with the drag queens and trannies taking the top floors. Chris lived on one of the bottom floors, in a narrow room with peeling wallpaper and a bankrupt bed. He lived little better than the homeless who pitched their cardboard shelters in Stuyvesant Park and in the doorframe of the nearby church. Chris endured it because he wanted to make a short film about the hotel and its tenants, but Marco guessed it was because Chris may have thought he was among the fabulous.

The guy at the desk was new. He wasn't the fat-faced blond boy who worked during the day or the weathered thirty-year-old manager. The new guy seemed to suffer from anemia or anorexia, had long knotted hair and silvery half-circles punched under his eyes, and he was about as useful as the moon. He wouldn't buzz Chris because it was past four in the morning and official visiting hours had ended at midnight.

"He's expecting me," Marco lied, more to himself than the desk guy.

He buzzed the room once. Then again. No answer.

Out on the steps, Marco tried to think of where he should go next, if anywhere. He didn't have the energy for an after-hours club or Patrick. If he wanted sex, he only had to walk back to Stuyvesant Park, wander the maze of benches and desiccated hedges, and wait under the pools of the sodium lamps. But he didn't want that. He was afraid he might run into Chris there. And all too suddenly, he didn't want Chris to find him either, not just in the park, but at the hotel, searching him out as if coming back on night's bruised knees. He flagged a cab and rode back to Midtown, to the hotel room he had rented for the weekend. It was easier than going home to his apartment after a late night at the theater.

He bought a cup of tea and a bagel at the deli across the street from his hotel and went up to his room. The Korean woman at the front desk usually gave him a crummy room with a burnt-out television and a dead radiator. He didn't care most times. The worse the room looked, the colder it felt, the easier it seemed to get the men out of there so he could make the next dance. This particular night, his room was warm, and he sat on the bed, cross-legged, eating and listening to the clanging radiator and the orders being shouted across the street on the loading docks of *The New York Times*. He fell asleep to those voices snarling over the speakers, voices spitting out directions to the trucks that would deliver the morning paper.

t w ●

From the train stop on Upper Broadway, the street on which Marco lived slid toward the Hudson River, diving past a block of high-rise apartments and prewar buildings, crossing West End Avenue and dropping further, past the Emily Dickinson Elementary School, its tiny garden, and an apartment building and then another and another. Marco lived in this last building, which, even in the flattering amber light of early afternoon, looked no better than what it was. It stood neglected and unadorned except for the dissolving stone lion carved over the cracked glass door.

He could smell his roommate Soledad's cigarette smoke as he climbed the dirty stairs and let himself into the top-floor apartment. Her bedroom door was closed. Sleeping, he hoped, and tried to shut the front door quietly, but it made a resounding smack as it settled into its frame. The linoleum squeaked as he crossed the dark hall toward his bedroom. He was startled to find Sol lying on the living room couch.

"Been out whoring again?" she asked, her bulk straining against a short negligee, a cheap satin horror she had bought from a mail-order catalog. He was surprised she wasn't flipping through the catalog now, tapping a fingernail against whatever grim seduction she might buy next. She sucked on her cigarette and squinted at him. "Where you been all weekend?"

"With a friend," Marco offered, hoping to say nothing more than that. He was tired and wanted to set down his backpack and get out of his clothes. They smelled too much of the theater.

Sol exhaled a fat stream of smoke. "Wha's his name again?"

"Chris."

"Yeah, tha's the one. You like 'im or somethin'?"

"He's all right, I guess," Marco said. He was never sure how he felt about Chris. His thoughts came off like petals from a daisy. He loved him. He loved him not. He loved him.

"You guess? Honey, you love 'im or you don't. It don't take no G.E.D."

"We used to be together. I don't know if I want to get back into it."

"I know what you mean, kid. I's only messing with you."

She convulsed with a tubercular laugh that soon became a shuddering choke. She struggled up from the couch, pounding her chest with her fist, and spit a wad of phlegm out the window. She lay back down, her breasts rolling to either side, heavy and worn as those that hung on the *cantineras* where Marco's father went drinking. Marco had never wanted to go, but his father could not leave the house unless he took Marco with him, and for hours Marco would wait in the parked El Camino or, when he got thirsty, at the bar drinking a Coke while his father slow-danced with the ruined women. *Cantineras, fulanas, huilonas,* his mother had all kinds of names for them, but even they looked like beauty pageant contestants against Sol.

The autumnal light flooding the living room made Sol vivid in a way no one needed. The corrosive black pits on her cheeks threatened to eat away the rest of her face. Her eyes were swollen, her squat nose smashed against her face, and her bleached-blond hair spiraled out, dry and broken as a cheap wig sold on

Fourteenth Street. Anytime Marco looked at her for too long, he got the urge to wash his face, scrub with a washcloth until his skin peeled away. This afternoon he only wanted to get to his room and slip into his shorts, run down to the reservoir in Central Park to take back his body, pull it back from the memory of all the calloused and dingy-nailed hands that had grabbed at him. He still felt their touch like a hungry troop of ants, carrying him down their little dark hole of nauseating pleasure.

Marco braced a smile against his face, more to deflect what he was thinking than to sympathize with Sol. He walked to his door and pushed into the room, leaving the door open as if he intended to return to the living room once he put his things down. Instead, he sat on the cold sheets of his bed and asked Sol if she'd had a good weekend. He did not care what she had done, but he felt he had to say something, and he half-listened to what she said, giving her the dismissive attention one gave people babbling to themselves on a subway train.

"I think this girl is the one," she said. "Miss Sixty-Thousand a Year." Marco heard her struggle up from the couch and was afraid she might come into his room, but then he heard the familiar click of her lighter. "Did I tell you about her?" She called out. "Works for the city like me. Doin' technical shit at the treatment plant over on Riverside. A man's job."

"I thought you were the butch one."

"Please." She laughed. "She paid for me to get my nails done this weekend. You shoulda seen it. They cost like twenty bucks. Now, no bitch I ever dated paid for no damned nails. I think I could do her for a while, you know? Get treated like a real woman." She sighed and the acrid zephyrs of smoke drifted into the bedroom. "I been with Yolanda too long, bein' her little side dish. I don't know what it's like to get treated like I's really am somebody. You know what I mean? Like a woman? The only woman! I hate sneaky shit. That ain' me."

Marco got up and stood at the door. He watched Sol take a final pull on her cigarette before grinding it into the window ledge and flicking it out. The smashed butt ricocheted off the bricks of the next building. She turned to him as she plugged another into her mouth. He flashed her another smile and told her he was going to close his door to keep the smoke from getting into his room. He forced a cough into his fist to make his point and shut the door. He grabbed a towel, ready to cover the gap underneath, but then he heard a groan, Sol heaving herself up from the couch, saying she would smoke in the kitchen.

When he first moved in, Sol claimed she only smoked in her bedroom. In the two years he had lived with her, she had smoked in every room of the apartment: in the kitchen as she cooked, in the living room watching television, and sitting on the toilet before she left for work at the unemployment office. She always had a cigarette in her hand or between her lips. Lying there on the couch, she must have burned through an entire pack.

Marco snapped open the blinds in his room, the plastic slats making a loud pop as they hit the window frames. He expected Sol to say something from the kitchen because she once told him to be careful with the blinds, they had cost her a fortune. She was always telling him what things cost her. The blinds may have been worth something at one time, but now they were discolored and warped. Even the window was cracked, the panes ready to shatter from the hard light pressing against them. He opened the window to clear the smoke already trapped in the room and the cold air shot through like flung knives. Last winter, a winter of debilitating record lows, Sol had lent him her electric heater, but he could only use it when most of the lights and all of the appliances were shut off. Otherwise the fuse blew.

He lived with Sol to save on cash and because there really was nowhere else to live. When he first moved to New York, he had lived with Chris at the hotel and scrolled through the classifieds of all the weeklies and searched the bulletin boards at laundromats and community centers and any place that might post a place for rent. Weeks passed and he never found anything he liked or could afford. He posted a room-wanted ad at the gay community center (YOUNG LATINO GAY MALE SEEKS ROOM) and expected a rich gringo to call and offer him the spare bedroom in his Central Park West apartment. That man never called. Sol called instead and Marco took her offer. For three hundred dollars, he knew he wasn't going to find anything better, at least nothing furnished. The room came with a narrow twin bed. A board sandwiched between the box spring and the mattress kept the bed from sagging in the middle. A raw wood vanity, which Sol called an antique, stood between two windows that led to a rear fire escape and faced the back of a huge apartment building.

Marco cracked the door open and yelled out into the hall that he was going to use the phone. If she heard him, Sol didn't answer. She was mad. He knew that but did not care.

He called his voice mail. Two messages. The first was left by Quentin who wanted to schedule a session for next Saturday. The second message was from Chris. Call him at the hotel. His voice, brittle from what Marco figured had been a late night, brought all the old feelings again, all familiar and tiring. He let the receiver rest against his chest. A return call would disturb things, the broken promises he had left buried, the resentments he did not want exhumed and resuscitated. He put the phone down and drew his running clothes from the bureau. Only three of the drawers worked. He imagined Sol considered the splintered pile an antique as well. In the silence, he could almost hear the rot spreading through the wood. Or was it the crackle of a call coming over the phone line? He picked up the receiver. The flat whine of the dial tone forced his hand. That was what he wanted to believe as he called the hotel. The blond boy (what was his name?) recognized him at once and put him through.

"Cristobál?" Marco felt his voice grope at the auditory blackness on the other end. At any moment, he expected the dial tone, the sure sign that Chris had hung up. When he still heard nothing, he went on and said, "*¿Hola? ¿Hola? ¿S'encuentra la señorita?*"

"*¿Yo?*" Chris asked, playing along in a thick and florid accent. "*Yo estoy muy buena.*"

For a moment, as the words churned through the chambers of his ear, Marco imagined Chris standing in a dark corridor at the hotel, the receiver between his red hair and thick shoulders. Marco could see him, but it didn't help him with what he should say next, how to navigate the gulf that had formed during the summer. The hot months had turned the paved streets into black canals and the canals had broken their banks and birthed a sea of obsidian desolation. Marco didn't know how to keep himself from going under, much less how to get across to where Chris now seemed anchored.

"So," Chris said, the word tossed like a safety line. "Was that you who came by at four this morning?"

"They told you I was there?"

"No. The front guy told me some cute boy came by looking for me. And I don't know too many cute boys. I figured it was you." His voice, pared down to the familiar strict diction, a clear enunciation of words, left Marco feeling as if he didn't know language. Chris seemed to always know exactly what to say and how. It was easy for him, as if he had rehearsed it a thousand times, scripted for yet another of his unmade movies. "You worked this weekend?"

"Yeah," Marco said, unsure if Chris really wanted to hear it, but perhaps he already knew. Chris seemed to know everything.

"Good weekend?" Chris asked.

"The usual."

"Yeah, right. You had them lined up the block."

"I wish. I'd use the money to get out of here."

"What?" Chris forced out a pinched laugh. "Out of that wonderful residence in the upper reaches of western Manhattan? Are her tampons plugging the toilet again?"

Marco laughed. This was the Chris he knew.

"You should've told me you were looking," Chris said, his words serious. "You should've said something. They've got doubles opening up here at the hotel. If we shared a room, you wouldn't pay any more than what you pay now."

"But then I gotta live with you again!" The phony banter soured. Marco tried to salvage the sinking moment with a joke. "I work hotels," he said, "I don't want to live in them."

"Well," Chris said, hesitating now, "I'm just putting that out. You do what you want."

"Thanks, but I was thinking something more final. I don't know. Like getting out of the city."

"Completely?" Chris asked. He paused. "I can't help you there.

I've become a hopeless New Yorker. I hate this city, but I can't imagine living anywhere else. You'll probably hear me moan about it for the next ten years."

That, Marco thought, was how he had felt about Chris. He wanted to shout to Sol to pick up the phone to listen. He did not hate Chris, but he did not love him, and living with him for the two years they had been together was about as satisfying as eating discarded cigarette butts and forcing out comments about how delicious the filters tasted and could he have more. For a while, neither Chris nor Marco said anything. They both knew they had reached the point in the conversation where the only thing left to do was hang up or ask each other out. Marco didn't want to be the one to ask because he was afraid Chris would say no. He would say no to punish him for not calling all those summer months. He felt the receiver heavy in his damp palms, the smell of smoke in the air, the scrape of feet lumbering down the hall.

"Are you free tonight?" Marco asked. The words were plain, almost right, but his voice sounded false to his own ears. The effort, he knew, would sink to the bottom of the silence between them. He tried again and exaggerated the shape of his words. "Are you free? Hello?"

"I'm not the working boy," Chris said.

"Tonight is my night off," Marco joked.

"So I guess anal sex is out of the question?"

Marco laughed a laugh of discomfort. "I'll be over at eight," he said, and then thought of being funny. "That should leave you enough time to tell the boy from last night to scram before I get there."

"Believe me, I've tried, but the kid is simply too in love with me. I'm telling you, that's the last time I go to the park." He paused to accommodate Marco's laughter, but it didn't come.

Chris had said those words to Marco before. He had been more serious then. And the words, which rang out like shots, startled a flock of cooped memories that scratched and clawed at Marco's throat. He repeated that he would see Chris at eight and hung up, swallowing hard, desperate for air.

Marco, changed into his shorts and running shoes, ran down the stairs and jogged up the street, a climb that reached all the way to Central Park. Once he crossed into the park, he slowed his pace, breathing deeply and adjusting his eyes to the bright leaves coloring the trees. The leaves were falling, swirling down in silent arabesques, curling and rolling along the dry grass in tight fists. Piles of them banked the chain-link fence surrounding the reservoir. He kicked a few into the air, pounding them back into the dirt track, and grabbed at the ones still clinging to the tree limbs. The other runners strode along, their knees braced, their tongues hanging out of their mouths like dogs, their headphones at full volume so that Marco could hear what they listened to. He preferred the metronomic pace of his own breath and the call of the birds floating on the water, the sound of the wind rushing past his ears, the thud of his feet. The city fell back then, blunted by the trees and the sky.

The sky blushed into evening and the distant apartment buildings soaked up the last rays of burnished light. Along the track, the lampposts fluttered open their insect eyes. Marco kept running, passing under the lamplight and the trees that formed a scarlet canopy like a Chinese New Year's dragon that had swallowed its tail.

He ran to get into his body, to both wake it up and tire it out, to feel it in a way that he never could with the johns, or anyone for that matter. On the days he didn't run, he felt dislocated and undone, which wasn't difficult with the way the city bore down on everyone. He had never run a lap before moving to New York. He was sure of it until a disparaging voice rose from the ground of that past buried and gone. It was Chris, of course, the enduring rankle of his voice keeping pace with Marco as he ran, needling him that they had gone running a few times in Houston. Marco could not remember the exact number of times, but he knew there were less than a handful, because he hated the whole ordeal of driving to the park, of looking for a spot for the car, of facing the evening traffic on the way home. No one did that in New York. No one drove to the reservoir. Or took a cab. Did they? In Houston he did not know about New York. He had just moved from Nowheres-burg and the glittering glass towers of the gas and oil companies of downtown Houston made him think he had finally arrived somewhere.

He was working as a cashier, at a diner in River Oaks, when he met Chris during a dinner break. The waitress was ignoring Marco, treating him the way she did bad tippers, probably spit-ting into his burger. As he sat in a booth, waiting for his food, Chris came in, wearing a pair of faded jeans and a billowy rust-colored shirt with too many buttons undone from the top. Sweat dripped off his upper lip, and with his pale brown eyes, he stared at Marco.

Marco looked down at the spotty silverware, wiping it with his napkin, making sure it was clean, the way he used to do in the other restaurant back home. Most of all, he wanted to avoid Chris, who was still looking at him. He didn't know Chris, but Chris sat at his table as if he did. He introduced himself and apologized for taking so long.

It took a few minutes to get the story down. Marco was not his blind date waiting for him at the diner. He hadn't answered a per-sonal ad in the newspaper. And his name was not Marco. That name would get adopted later.

He told Chris his real name, the accents wrung out of it like a dish towel, done to help Chris, but Chris repeated his name in an exaggerated tone. He sounded like the gringa Spanish teacher from high school.

Chris motioned for the waitress to bring him a glass of water. He drained it to its scummy bottom and then excused himself to use the pay phone. He returned to the table muttering and offering further apologies. The waitress popped her gum and asked him if he was going to sit his cute ass down and order. She batted her eyes. Chris looked at Marco and then back at the waitress and asked for whatever Marco was having. He sank back into the booth, his face red from the heat outside or embarrassment, though Marco was beginning to think that Chris never felt ashamed about anything.

Marco said nothing. He listened to this strange new guy complain about the traffic-choked freeways. He cursed the hot weather and the busted air conditioner in his car. He cooled down once the food came. And by the end of the meal, he had invited Marco to the cabaret show he had planned to take the other guy to that night, but Marco couldn't go. He had to finish his shift. He wouldn't be done until midnight. Chris said he understood and left after he finished his meal. Marco thought nothing more would happen. He didn't expect to find Chris in the parking lot at midnight, sitting on the hood of his car, his eyes fired by the neon framing the diner windows.

There was more. Definitely, there was more about Chris, maybe too much, but the sky over the reservoir was dark now and Marco had to return to his apartment before heading downtown. He inhaled deeply, letting the chill air fill his lungs. His heart missed a beat when another runner passed, his headphones leaking a song familiar to him from the theater. He didn't have to go back there for at least another two weeks or until he needed money again. He tried to put the theater out of his mind, but the yank at his memory had begun and everything unraveled: the hollowed-out men he had seen that weekend, the sanatized stink of the hotel, the fatigue wrapped tight around his bones. He pulled at the memories, running his hands down his limbs and across his torso. He pulled and tore at all that had troubled him, crumpled them up and flung the remains under a bush, into the trees, or over the fence and into the calm waters of the reservoir where he imagined they might dissolve. He tore at the next layer and the next until he had stripped down to his real self. He lost himself to himself, his hips aching, his legs tight and slick, the sweat rolling down to quench the heat in the soles of his feet.

He turned onto the final stretch of track and then slowed to a walk before he stopped and grabbed at the cold chain-link fence, steadying his breath, looking out over the water to the linear constellation of lights from the lampposts. In the distance, out toward Central Park West, a warm light burned in the window of a cupola anchored to a massive apartment building. It was the kind of fantastic place in which he always wanted to live.

A funky dance version of a torch song played through the bar. Marco sat on a corner stool at the rear. Chris, who seemed to have gained a few pounds, a thick roll pressing against his shirt, sat beside him and lit a cigarette. The burst of the match threatened to ignite his red hair, but he remained unmoved and let the pale smoke encircle him like a feather boa as he exhaled.

Chris had always been a better drag queen than boyfriend. That was what Marco thought. He didn't want to care anymore, and told himself he shouldn't and wouldn't. What had remained of their relationship had been extinguished months ago. He said this to himself now, as he had many times before, to reassure himself, to have it firmly posted in the landscape of his mind. He didn't want regret shadowing his thoughts. Their life together had dive-bombed early last summer when Chris flew to Berlin with one of his johns. Chris said he was quitting the business and the trip was to be the last of it. He had asked Marco to quit with him. Marco wouldn't. He hadn't had his trip to Berlin yet. If not Berlin, then Amsterdam, or Paris. All the guys at the theater talked about being flown to Paris for the weekend. The only places Marco had been were Baltimore and a few snowy villages upstate.

The boys at this particular bar didn't seem to go anywhere beyond Times Square. With their baggy clothes and the gold charms hanging off their necks and set into their ears and teeth, the boys working here seemed trapped by the hard neon. The bar had go-go boys, as did every other bar or club, but none of them stripped nude like at the theater where Marco danced. Not one guy came out with a hard-on. Here the guys danced, stripped to a g-string, and worked the crowd for tips or made appointments for later. Chris said he liked this bar for the grit. It made him think that the theater, at least when he had worked there, was the top of a mercenary heap. The bar never made Marco feel he was at the top of anything. It only made him see how easily he could lose work to the guys who went for less.

Marco ordered some red wine and asked for it in a cocktail glass. In a bar like this one, wine glasses looked stupid and fragile to him, but the bartender forgot about the cocktail glass, and

Marco stared at his wine with disappointment.

"I shouldn't be ordering wine anyway," he complained. "Not in here. It's probably so cheap I'll get a purple ring around my mouth."

"It might be good for business." Chris motioned to the bartender.

"I'm not taking any money tonight."

"Does this mean I get it free?" Chris said, wearing a loose smirk, a transparent nightie ready to drop to the floor. He turned to the bartender and asked for an empty glass, pointing to his own glass of gin.

When he had the empty glass in his hand, Chris dumped the wine into it without spilling a single bruised drop. He cocked his head and puckered his lips, as if expecting applause, a pose Marco had seen too many times, the entire snap of movements hitting marks meant to seduce. Most people found it charming. Marco had once too, but after years of watching the same choreography he thought it contrived and pathetic. He took a sip of his wine to flush out the bitter knot he felt in his throat, but the wine only left a sour trail down to the pit of his stomach. He regretted coming.

"How's business?" Chris asked. "Make the quota this weekend?"

"Barely," Marco said, not wanting to talk about it.

"Don't give me that. You had them lined up from here to Miami."

"And you? You really quit or were you just trying to impress me?"

"Baby, there ain't nothing impressive about going broke." Chris took a swallow of his drink and looked around the bar. His eyes, with their muddled browns, seemed as comforting and protective as the buttons on a favorite winter coat. He had no trace of makeup, which was unusual, since he proclaimed all life cinema. (You needed the concealers and powders and charcoal pencils for those damned closeups, he insisted.) Marco liked him denuded like this, not a drag-ball queen, but an aged pretty boy.

"What happened to your job at the television studio?" Marco prodded.

"Still got it. But I work twice as hard for less money." On his lips, a grim smile seesawed. "It's such a shock to go back into the real world and try to survive on piss wages and do such uninteresting work. Stay young and beautiful."

"You don't miss it?"

"What?" Chris grunted. "The business? Do I miss the business?" He seemed to think about it. "I miss the money. Not the men."

"And Richard?"

"What about Richard?" he asked, as if bored.

"Are you still seeing him?"

"He calls when he's in town. Which isn't often nowadays. He's having trouble with his business. The bastard went bankrupt. He spent too much."

"On you," Marco said, taking a sip of his wine.

"Oh, it wasn't me. I didn't take all his money."

"I thought you were moving with him to England."

"Good thing I didn't. He's losing the cottage."

"You really left him dry."

"I don't want to talk about him. He's so uninteresting to me now. I don't know how I spent so much time with him. I guess I was being social."

"The guy was in love with you."

"Please," Chris shot out in a frustrated rush, "he wasn't in love with me. I told him not to be. I told him I was in love with some-one else."

"There's always someone else."

"Don't get all defensive. I was talking about you." Chris turned to him with his practiced smile. "And don't look at me like you just spilled out from between your mother's legs."

"I thought we went over this already."

"Oh we did," Chris said. His smile disappeared, like a street hawker hiding his contraband, ready to try his luck elsewhere.

Marco turned away, wanting another sip of wine, but hating the taste of its bitter bouquet of soured grapes. He had always doubted Chris and his pronouncements of love. There always seemed to be someone else. Marco searched the bar to see who that might be tonight, but all the men were turned to the pool game where a drag queen crouched over the table, cue stick in hand, lining up the balls for a straight shot.

"Does it surprise you?" Chris asked, his words as crushed as cigarette butts. "In Berlin, you'll be happy to know, I made Richard miserable. We'd be out on the balcony of the penthouse he had rented and I'd tell him how much I missed you. He offered to fly you in for a weekend. I would have told him to go ahead with it if I thought you'd come, but I knew how much you hated him."

"I would have gone," Marco lied.

"You would." Chris said it more as an accusation than a question.

"I've never been to Berlin."

"You hated Richard."

"I didn't hate him," Marco said, not knowing exactly what he felt. He paused. "I felt sorry for him, I guess. I knew you were going to break the old man's heart after you got back from your trip."

"You broke mine."

"As if you didn't have a stable of other boys ready to take my place." Marco knew he was exaggerating, though not lying. He stared at Chris, navigating the murk in his eyes, at the past that seemed to whorl and tilt in them like an obscene carnival ride. "Men are like potato chips to you. You just can't have one. You eat the whole bag."

"Don't tell me what I need."

"Okay, so you enjoy it."

"It's flattering."

"For you, maybe," Marco shot back. "I can't live with it."

"Am I supposed to wear a set of blinders? Is that what you want?"

"What I want," Marco started to say, but his words dropped off with the rise in music, with the crescendo of rattling electronic tambourines and the steady beat of a drum. He knew he didn't have to defend himself or listen to any more excuses or make a plan that would keep them together. It was over for them. He didn't want anything. He didn't want anything from Chris.

Marco looked at him. Why fight, he thought. They should treat one another as friends, or at least with a modicum of respect, though he remembered the last time he had called, Chris had turned down his invitation to dinner. Marco asked Chris if he remembered it. "I was passed up for what's his name?"

"Nathan." Chris stifled a laugh and then asked the guy next to him for a cigarette and a light. "Nathan has a lover, you know. They've been living together for ten or eleven years. They've got rent control and everything. They're never going to break up."

"So what's the point in seeing him?"

"Not everything has to have a point," Chris said sourly. "Everything doesn't have to be something. I don't think I could live if everything was of some great importance. That's one thing I've learned in this city. The less something matters, the better."

"So you're settling."

"Baby, this girl is not settling." Chris took a hard pull on his cigarette. "Settling would be sitting at home waiting for Nathan to land at the hotel like some sweepstakes prize. I still manage to have a good time."

"You're seeing other people," Marco said, sure of it.

"Whoever I come across at the peep booths, the park, wherever."

"Quality material."

"Like you never go, Sister of the Immaculate Infection." Chris stubbed out his unfinished cigarette and seemed desperate to ask the guy for another, if not just help himself to the pack lying on the bar. "Anything else you want to know?"

"I was just asking."

"So ask," Chris erupted. "Just stop being so damned smug."

"I only wanted to ask about Nathan."

"You've said that."

"I thought he liked you."

"He does." He glared at Marco and then let his eyes search the room. "He tells me all the time."

"And you're seeing other people?"

"What does it matter?" he almost shouted, his face turned to Marco.

"I'm sure it matters to Nathan. Don't you think he should know about the other guys? About Richard?"

"I'm not seeing Richard. I told you. And the thing between Nathan and me is not that simple. We've been through a lot in the past year."

"I thought you just met him."

"I met him a year ago."

"A year ago you were still trying to go to bed with me."

"A year ago you were still saying no."

Marco turned away. He wondered what Chris was not telling him now. Chris had always accused him of being insular and uncommunicative because he never expressed his feelings well. But Chris communicated his feelings too well, saying he loved Marco, wanted him, whatever, and then went out and cheated on him, crushing everything he had said and promised. Sure, Marco couldn't tell Chris every hour of the day that he loved him, or buy him flowers, or chocolates, much less take him on a fabulous trip through Europe, but he never gave up. He never went out on him. Marco paused for a moment. He hadn't realized until now, perhaps because Chris had always been quick to point out Marco's mistakes and shortcomings to justify his own failings, but for Marco, a successful relationship was about nothing more than not giving up. He looked at his nearly empty glass, not remembering having drank any of it.

"You never wanted a relationship," Marco mumbled in a voice strangled by the cruel-fisted past. "Not like you told me. You never meant a word of it."

"Fine," Chris said.

When he heard Chris say it, not so much an admission that he was right, but a surrender of defeat, Marco knew he had pushed too far. He regretted having said anything, but he couldn't deny that he was still hurt. He thought he had put the misery behind him.

Chris excused himself to go to the bathroom. Marco took a final sip of his wine. It tasted awful and he felt bits of the cork stick to his throat. He set the glass down and tried to see back to the beginning, to the diner at the midnight hour when he found Chris in the parking lot, sitting on the hood of his car. Chris had come back to see him and asked if he would sit in his car for a few minutes, and once inside, begged for a kiss. At first, Marco moved away from him, gripping the door, almost pushing himself out of the car. He was afraid someone in the diner would see them. He didn't want them to know he was gay. He thought it would get him fired. He told Chris that this was why he wouldn't kiss him, but Chris, with an impatient insolence, told Marco that everyone at the diner probably already knew. He said it with the authoritative tone of a television news anchor, with a canned laugh and bleached smile, all metered speech and modulated voice, intelligent, charming. Marco believed him and leaned over the sweaty stick shift to kiss him. After weeks of proposals, he agreed to move in with him. He had never lived with anyone other than his parents. It proved to be as difficult.

He still wanted his freedom. Not the freedom for sex with a lot of different men, but the freedom from being needed, from having to be someone for someone else, from being responsible for their happiness. He had suffered enough, dancing with his mother, his father banking on him as a future breadwinner. With Chris it was only a slight variation on the same song and dance. (Instead of Agustin Lara, it was now Annie Lennox.) Chris had arrogated him and seemed to hold him accountable for every ensuing moment. Every delight depended on him and every disappointment seemed pinned to him, and the weight of it all made him resent Chris with a debilitating fury that only crippled his passion. Was he not supposed to love Chris? Chris claimed to love him. He was always claiming his love, but Marco always refused to believe it, for a lot of reasons. For one thing, he knew Chris was a flirt. He approached everyone with an almost illicit interest. He dressed in the barest suggestions of clothes and subscribed to porn magazines, one of which he had posed for at nineteen. He claimed to have had more one-night stands than he could count. Marco was afraid he had become engaged to the town slut. He kept imagining Chris with other guys. Marco had never been with anyone other than Chris.

What made things more difficult was that Chris worked late nights at a posh hotel and didn't come home until two or three in the morning. Chris said he liked being the last one home because then he would find Marco already asleep, in their bed, which made him happy. Waking up together should have been enough to keep Marco secure, to know that Chris hadn't spent the night elsewhere, but something in him refused to let go. In the mornings, he'd eye Chris suspiciously until the alarm went off and Chris skimmed the waking surface for a few moments before slipping back under like a corpse disappearing into a bayou. Marco checked Chris's clothes for strange hairs and his pockets for phone numbers. As a kid, late at night, Marco would lie in his bed, listening to his mother examine his father's clothes as his father snored. She would mumble to herself that his father had been good, so good at hiding all the things she knew he was out doing.

Looking long and hard enough, Marco eventually found what he wanted to find: two shit-stained condoms floating in the toilet. Neither one of which Marco remembered using. They hadn't had real sex in a while. When confronted, Chris blamed him for driving him to it. Marco congratulated himself for knowing better than to have fallen stupid in love, but it still hurt, and he cried in the shower, where Chris could not see him, and he searched the downtown districts for another place to live. The worst part of not having an immediate place to go, since he had no family, no friends, was listening to Chris phone other guys and arrange to go out with them. Chris was going on with his life. When he started stripping at a nearby bar for contest money, Marco felt so raw with jealousy and curiosity that he couldn't leave. He unpacked. They stayed together a year and moved to New York to live in the middle of everything. They both thought the added hardship of making a living in the big city would bring them closer together. It did for a while. They shared a room at Hotel Seventeen. Chris went to film school and began dancing at the theater after going to an audition posted in the *Village Voice*. Marco went soon after. He did not want another restaurant job and he did not want Chris to think he was terrified or weaker somehow. For Marco, going with the men for private shows wasn't any more terrible than dancing naked, or suffering the act of sex with Chris, who he had not wanted for a long time.

When Chris returned from the bathroom, walking past the abandoned pool game, his eyes ringed with a red dampness, Marco apologized, though he didn't know for what, since it wasn't

34

as if he had accused him of anything that couldn't be circum-
stantiated. Chris told him to forget about it, his head thrown back
in a strong snap, and turned to the strippers. Marco shut up and
watched the show. The boys danced under the hot lights, sweat
beading on their upper lips and bare chests, matting the hair
under their arms. They looked like the roughnecks who played
basketball by the West Fourth Street subway stop, an entire naked
squad of them without a ball or blacktop.

"How long you want to stay?" Chris asked.

"Doesn't matter," Marco said, suppressing a yawn. The thought
of taking the train home, to a room quartered by the cold, left him
without direction and despondent.

Out on the sidewalk, the wind bit hard and damp. If lying alone,
shivering under his thin covering of sheets didn't depress him so
much, Marco would've returned home. He wouldn't have gotten
into a cab with Chris to ride back to Seventeen.

Matchbooks with scrawled names and phone numbers were
scattered around the room. Clothes were in a soiled mound in
one corner. Marco sat on the edge of the narrow bed to untie his
shoes and found a used condom stuck to the floor under the
nightstand. A framed photo of him was propped against the
lamp. Chris had taken it at their old apartment in Houston. In the
monochromatic scene of heather blue-blacks and dull whites,
Marco was seated, looking at himself in a large mirror. His knees
were up, and pressed against his chest were a bunch of daisies,
soft as cake decorations. One flower dangled from behind his
ear. His face was unsmiling, though calm, lips full, forehead
aglow. He looked younger than the nineteen he had been in the
photo. That was what Chris had insisted from behind the camera. Chris had made him feel good then. Those first days, when
they were getting to know each other, Chris took him to the bars
and dance clubs and introduced him to all his friends. The world
was huge and good and Marco felt he was going to have a part
in it after all, which he had always hoped, but never could imagine. Marco remembered that now.

Chris switched off the lights and climbed into bed. Marco

moved toward the wall, afraid any contact would lead to sex, but wanting to be held, to remember every recorded moment dug up from the shoe-boxed past. Even the bad moments gave rise to a sympathetic warmth, as if memories, whatever their content, were good just because he had them. In his gathering sleep, he walked through that huge apartment in Houston, the two bedrooms, the separate kitchen, the dining area that spilled into the living room where the camera and the lamps had been set up for the shoot. The apartment was the size of an entire floor at Seventeen, and the walls had smooth pastel coats of paint instead of ragged wallpaper, and the sliding glass doors overlooked an oak-shaded courtyard with a pool. At Seventeen, the windows in the rooms, if there were any, opened on rusting fire escapes and the monochromatic stone faces of the neighboring buildings.

Morning was still hours away, the sky a stubborn dark, when Marco woke up with the odd weight of Chris's hand on his crotch.

"What are you doing?" Marco whispered to him.

The hand went limp and Chris yawned in a horrible charade of waking up. He mumbled, "What's going on?"

"You were having a bad dream," Marco said, punching him in the shoulder.

"Ouch." Chris laughed.

Marco reached over and massaged the bruised shoulder. He let his hand move down the meaty arm to entwine with Chris's cool fingers. He let them rest a moment and then brought both of their hands back onto his underwear. He let Chris touch him, stroke him in a way that was familiar to them both. For Marco, it was good to be with someone who knew him, knew how to please him, but he pushed Chris away when he tried to go down on him. Marco didn't have to say anything. Chris should have known, from all the nights they had worked together, that Marco abstained from real sex for a day or two after a weekend at the theater. He either wasn't in the mood or was afraid he had contracted a disease from one of the johns. He didn't want to infect anyone else. Still, Chris groaned with disappointment. Marco spit into his hands and reached for Chris, forgetting about

Nathan and the other guys. Were there other guys? He couldn't remember. They came, Marco and Chris, and then drifted back to sleep, to the sound of rain running off the slate roof of the church across the street.

three

The fall leaves hung bright and sharp, as if cut from construction paper and pasted on the tree limbs by school children. The leaves fluttered with an occasional wind, teasing them with the miracle of flight, but it was not until the heavy rains of the season brought them down, staining the world with their rust-colored streaks. The wet leaves choked the gutters and carpeted the sidewalks where the torn ticket stubs of summer lay disintegrating underneath. Gone were the early mornings when Marco lay in bed with the weight of the first rays across his chest like the arm of a lover he no longer loved but still missed. Gone were the tasteless noon sandwiches he made for himself and ate on the roof of his building, listening for the call of the barges on the Hudson, some days hoping for the slightest breeze. Gone too were the nights he spent at Theater 80 on St. Mark's where he watched marathon runs of old movies to escape the heat and streets wet with perspiration. Those long days of summer, days that seemed suffocated by the hours, those days were closing, their light dying.

Now he found himself consumed by the leaves, their fire something to be pressed between the pages of a book. He had done that his first year in the city, filled an entire hardcover novel with the leaves he collected, and had the urge to do it now, as he drifted through the days, like a leaf suspended in the chill air. He felt himself buoyed. He had regained a sense of himself. The part he had lost had come back to him with Chris now at his side. They passed down East Village streets with their arms flung across each other's shoulders and held hands under the candlelit tables of Italian restaurants and in the brash lights of the greasy diners near Hotel Seventeen. (Chris's favorite was Little Poland on Second Avenue. He loved their cheese babka and the high-pitched whine in which the waitresses pronounced it.) They went wherever Chris wanted. Marco was giving himself over, or so he thought, until he began to realize that Chris never seemed satisfied. If Marco met one of his demands, Chris had others.

To placate the complaint that he never planned an evening for them, that he didn't care enough about the two of them, Marco began taking the lead, as Chris once did, but Chris would sulk that he didn't like the restaurant Marco had picked, or the movie, or the bar. Marco felt he couldn't do anything right. Anything he did was met with a groan, a reprimand, a verbal assault. It was as if he still did all the things Chris had complained about in the past. Marco knew he had changed, though, and tried to do better, wanting to show Chris how good a boyfriend he had become. Chris never seemed to think so and there was no way to convince him otherwise. He seemed to want to keep Marco as the boyfriend he once knew, an angry little wonder trapped in amber, a specimen even Marco found, when he looked back, a bit unsettling.

So while the first few days of their reunion had raged like a bonfire (but weren't the flames nothing more than the leaves in the trees?), the following weeks burned down to a dry pile of ash. Their faces hardened and conversation, if they spoke at all, blew itself out into swirling flakes of quiet resentment. Silence now colored once-bright days black.

Marco figured ways in which to escape the familiar complaints and Chris altogether, because it became as naked to him as the trees outside, that Chris would never be able to see him for who he was now. Chris was unwilling to separate him from who he had been once. In his eyes, Marco had not changed, and could not, perhaps. Life might always be as they had known it, drafted with petty arguments and staged with cheerless backdrops and brittle props.

At the hotel, just one of the sets in which the drama with Chris was now and forever playing out, Marco went through the preparations for a weekend of dancing. He brushed his teeth and deoderized while Chris searched the cluttered room for the electric shears. Marco was surprised he had offered to help at all, but then they had always helped each other the weekends they both worked at the theater. They took turns shaving each other smooth, because Chris insisted there was nothing more unattractive than a hairy ass or an overgrown thicket of pubic hair. Shaved clean, he thought they looked younger and almost virginal.

Chris plugged in the shears, their steel teeth buzzing angrily. He pulled Marco over to a piece of newspaper spread on the floor and pushed his legs open wide.

"It might hurt a little," Chris said over the noise of the machine. "They're rusty."

He crouched in front of Marco, moving the shears over the inside of his thighs. They tugged and yanked at the hair. Marco gritted his teeth. Chris continued shaving until the shears pulled again. Marco jerked back and pressed his lips into a grim line to keep from crying.

"I'm sorry," Chris said, his voice low and focused. "You think Vaseline might help?"

"I don't have time," Marco replied. "Just be more careful."

"All right, but don't blame me if you get razor bumps."

"I had a huge one right in the crack of my ass a few weeks ago." Marco tried to get his mind off the pain around the inside of his thighs. "It hurt to sit down."

"You sure that wasn't a wart?"

"No, it wasn't a wart, thank you very much. It had puss in it."

"Could have been herpes," Chris said under his breath.

"Herpes doesn't get that big."

"You know what it looks like?"

"Last time I went to the clinic, a counselor tried to scare me with his book, full-color photographs of all the sexually transmitted diseases you could ever want."

Marco's dick was limp from the pain of the shears. He pulled his balls up so that Chris could get between his legs. He shut his eyes, anticipating the pain, concentrating on the soft beats coming from the leak in the sink. It sounded like the lingering quiet after a fierce rain. Then he felt a warm mouth.

"What are you doing?" Marco asked.

Chris mumbled something.

Marco pulled back, bringing Chris stumbling forward, wiping his lips.

"I have to work tonight," Marco complained. "I can't do this."

"Do what?"

"Have sex with you."

"And if I threw in a few bucks?" Chris shot up from the floor.

"You don't have enough," Marco said, no trace of humor in his voice.

He pulled on his underwear, his shaven crotch prickly against the cotton. The scratchiness made him aware of his dick. Tonight at the theater, he would be stroking himself to the music, showing himself to hundreds of strange men. They didn't care about anything else. It was as if dick was all he was.

He put on his clothes and wadded up the newspaper, stuffing it into the small garbage can spilling over with greasy take-out containers. Chris moved to a corner of his bed, his face to the window, as if Marco was not there anymore. Marco grabbed his backpack. He didn't know what to say, if anything. He was afraid of leaving, that this might be his last time at the hotel, which was what he had hoped for, an escape, but now he wasn't sure he was ready to walk out the door. Chris came over and put his arms around him, holding him tight.

"Let go," Marco whispered. "I'm gonna be late."

"Don't go." Chris pressed closer as if to push through and get inside.

"I have to go."

"You don't have to."

"I told them I'd be there. I have to go."

"You don't have to," Chris repeated, pushing himself away. His face broke apart with fury and he stood stiffly, challenging Marco before retreating to the bed. "You don't have to do this."

"But you did," Marco said defensively.

"I was putting myself through school. I had to do it."

"No. You wanted to."

"I had to pay tuition, living expenses, and find time to study. I had no choice," Chris said. "Now I have a degree, but what do you have? I don't see you working toward anything, nothing that's going to get you anywhere. So, why do it? For what? For rent? And what is that? Three hundred dollars a month? You could pay that with a regular job and still have money for everything else. You don't need to be doing this."

Down the hall, in one of the communal bathrooms, a shower started and its hiss accompanied the leak from the sink, the drops of water sending up lazy soft beats.

"Quit," Chris said, his voice soft, like a word he did not want to say. "You can move in with me or we can find an apartment together. We'll start over. It'll be different. I'm serious. Don't go tonight."

"They need me at the theater."

"I need you," he mumbled. "I don't want you to go there."

"And you're going to pay my bills?"

"I'll do it if it means getting you out of there."

Marco had forgotten how generous Chris could be. When they went out to dinner, Chris sometimes offered to pay the entire check, something Marco never did. Chris bought him flowers for no reason. He even treated Marco to a Broadway show a couple times. The tickets were bought at the discount ticket booth in Times Square, but Marco never would have considered, in his earlier life at least, taking Chris to anyplace more extravagant than a movie.

"I don't want you dancing there anymore," Chris repeated. His face seemed pieced back together by calm. "We'll rewrite your résumé, you know, fix it up here and there, lie if we have to. I can help you. You got offers from a few places last time. You can get a real job. The theater is no good for you."

"Oh, now it's not good for me," Marco sneered and made a grab for the door. He paused. "Tell me, how does it feel to know everything?"

"Stop acting like a child."

"Isn't that what you want? A charity case to depend on you for everything?" Chris remained silent. Marco had always suspected, ever since meeting him, that Chris wanted to keep him dumb as the dishwasher he had once been, a boy concerned with nothing more than scraping the baked cheese off an enchilada plate. Then Marco would be forced to see Chris as the dazzling savior with the flaming crown of red hair. Chris wanted to keep him enthralled, so beaten by his theatrics that he was perpetually and pathetically awed and grateful. All he could manage tonight was a stagnant disgust.

He waited for Chris to do something, make some grand pronouncement or gesture worthy of an aging and bitter actress, but Chris stayed motionless and quiet. "I'll see you later," Marco said, opening the door. "I have work to do."

"Thanks to me," Chris added.

"Yeah," Marco said, the sour note suspended in the air. "Thanks to you I have this fabulous life."

Chris stood up from the bed. "If it weren't for me," he said, taking a hesitant step forward. "If it weren't for me, you wouldn't be the person you are now."

Marco tightened his grip on the doorknob, grounding himself against the bolting pain of being reminded of who he was and whom he owed. Before Chris, he had belonged to his parents. But his parents were never his. He was always theirs. Their son, their *hijo*. His father reminded him of it with every word he spoke. He had them all, *las cuatas, el negro,* but especially him, he'd say, to help him in his old age, to work for him and bring money home. Marco was an investment, like his mother had been to her father, working cotton fields faster than any of her brothers. Her father begrudgingly let her marry. He didn't want to give her away because she was his "best mule." This was what Marco's father claimed. This was what the man who bore Marco told him on nights as jagged and threatening as smashed beer bottles. He smelled of piss and cigarettes, the kitchen of reheated food and store-bought tortillas, the *colonia* of the milky weeds and mangy dogs that curled up on the dirt road to sleep. Marco did not want to belong to this life, or to the man who had brought him into it, or to anyone other than himself. All he had to do, he imagined then and tonight at the hotel, was walk out the door. And go where? And alone? He gripped the knob tighter and looked at Chris, who had come a few steps closer. "Maybe it's time I let you find some other lucky boy to ruin," Marco said. "Marry a whore and see the world."

Chris smiled. "Baby, I'm not the one working tonight."

"No, you're right," Marco said, loosening his hold on the door, a short snap of air pushing out of his nostrils. "But at least this whore can still sell it. You couldn't even give it away."

The sink stopped leaking and the shower hissing. Everything evaporated to a dull gasp, as if the plumbing in the entire hotel had gone dry. Chris seemed to suffer from it too, his face stripped to bone, and breaking. Marco knew he had gone too far. This would be the end of it, the final blow in which everything shattered in too many places, too difficult to pick up and piece back together again. He waited for Chris to say something. He felt as if he had said too much already.

"I don't like this," Chris grumbled. "I don't like that this is still going on."

"What's going on?" Marco let go of the door and folded his arms.

"Oh please."

"What?"

"Nothing has changed, all right. You say it's over, just like you always say it's over, but you still come around or call or whatever it is you do. If you want this to end, then end it. Stop coming here. Stop calling. Stop giving me this stupid hope."

Marco swallowed. "I just don't want to hurt your feelings."

"You don't want to hurt my feelings?" Chris choked down his tears with a laugh. "You've already hurt my feelings, many, many

45

times. Maybe you don't want to hurt your own feelings." He moved to the window and kept his face turned away from Marco, but Marco knew, by the way his voice trembled, that he was crying. "You know," Chris said, "I can't be here for you every time you need me. I only take you back because I'm just as selfish as you are. But I can't do it anymore." Chris wiped his eyes. When he turned back to Marco, he looked exhausted, extinct. "You're going to be late," he said.

Marco wanted to say he didn't care about being late. Right now he cared more about whether Chris was going to be all right. He regretted what he had said. It always came to this emotional back-and-forth when he was close to losing Chris. His confusion came from knowing that life with Chris made sense. It should have worked, but never did. Still, he could never get over the idea that what they had made together, what they knew about each other, and what they had learned, had to be abandoned. He wasn't as ready to walk away from Chris as he thought.

He was about to move toward him when the church bells from Stuyvesant Park struck the hour. It was late. It was too terribly late. He said Chris's name from where he stood but Chris refused to look at him. He thought the squeak of the door, as he opened it, would bring Chris rushing to him, but it didn't even so much as earn him a glance. Marco slipped out the room and headed down the dark corridor to the elevator. As he waited for the doors to open, a loud thud reverberated against the walls behind him. Chris, he knew, liked to hit things.

Marco rushed up the hard-lit stairs to the theater box office. Esther passed him the key without bothering to look up from the magazine she was reading. He unlocked the exit door and slipped the key back behind the window and said thank you, but Esther waved him off, her face masked by a spill of dark hair.

Inside, the theater stank of sweaty crotches and stale cologne. Marco adjusted the weight of his backpack and, for a single moment, thought he should turn around and hurry back down the stairs and onto the street. He had to leave this place with all its firebox smells, but hearing the muffled play of music, a strained lyric of an unfamiliar song, Marco waded through the musty heat to the DJ both where Manuel sat reading a celebrity tabloid with Madonna on the cover. Manuel worshipped her. The walls of the booth were plastered with posters and magazine cut-outs and pages from her photo book on sex. She had dedicated a section of the book to the theater and photographed herself with a couple of dancers. The prints hung framed in the lounge.

"I didn't know she could still make news," Marco said. He knew it would set Manuel off.

"Mi amor."

"¿Que dice la pobre?"

"Aye, tu sabes, trabajando commo una negra."

Marco laughed. He liked Manuel and his blunt humor. Chris never had anything nice to say about him, not since Manuel told him that he needed to lose a few pounds. The message was supposed to have come from Olga, the theater manager, but Chris thought Manuel was just being hateful. In any case, Manuel was the DJ, and was entrusted with keeping the show moving. Marco asked, "You got my music lined up?"

"¿Asi es?" Manuel slapped down the paper. "Use me for the music."

"I was hoping to get my song again before anyone else got it."

"Mi amor, I'm not gonna play that song again. *Coño,* last week we auditioned three new girls and they all asked for that song. I nearly scratched the record *para terminar ese pedo que tienen atorado."*

"Could they dance at least?"

"¡Aye no! There was one who even came in a policeman's uniform with the Velcro pants. I guess she thought this was Chippendale's." Manuel turned in his seat and pulled out a record from the stack he had lined up for that night's show. "You know we got something from this *hija puta."*

"Who?" he asked, setting his pack down.

"Pues quien mas."

Manuel set the record on the turntable and passed Marco the headset. The song came out in thick notes. It seemed too slow for a first song, but Marco listened anyway, waiting for the L-word

47

and any other pathetic lyric that would disqualify it.

Through the square hole that looked out on the stage, he imagined himself dancing, almost placing himself in the "Open Your Heart" video in which Madonna danced on a similar glittery stage, the men watching from inside coin-operated booths. He had always wondered about the kind of money a dancer like that could make. Was it a living? Was this?

At the theater, in the envelope of cash he received at the end of the weekend, he never counted more than a hundred dollars. Of course, he tapped the johns for more, but he never let himself need them too much. He never tried to see too many of them, otherwise he felt about as tossed around as the trinkets at the souvenir shops in Times Square.

When he practiced his dance routine at home in front of the vanity, Marco pictured the men flashing fifty-dollar bills, contorting their faces into ridiculous expressions of ecstasy, their eyes rolling into wheels of color from the lights reflected off his bare skin. Onstage he would push his body against the shiny back curtain, stick his ass out and look back over his shoulder at the men, and then drop to his hands and knees and crawl down the stage ramp where the men were lined up alongside. He smiled at the older men with their raincoats shrouding their laps, at the younger buff ones who hung back, their feet up against the seats, watching him like a movie they'd picked out of the video store, unsure if they liked it. He took everyone in, even those men leaning against the far walls and those by the doors. The luckiest man of them all sat at the end of the ramp. Some nights Marco had to convince himself of that about everyone. It was the only way he could make it out onto the stage at all. He had to believe he was beautiful and that they wanted him. He didn't have the patience or the energy or the attitude to hustle. He also felt he didn't have the face. He wouldn't have paid to have sex with himself. He danced because he wanted to know if he was as ugly as he thought or as beautiful as he desperately wanted to be.

"*¿Te gusta?*" Manuel asked, pulling out other records.

Marco nodded, taking off the headset and handing them back.

"It's fine," he said. "I think I have to hear it a few times to get into it. I don't know why, but that's how it is with most of her songs. I never like them in the beginning."

"Bueno no me vas á contar más tarde," Manuel said, slipping the record onto a stack of others. *"Si quieres otra vaina, mi amor, me dices. ¿Bueno?"*

Marco nodded and grabbed his pack before stepping out of the booth. He could never hold his side of the conversation when Manuel slipped into his Venezuelan Spanish. The words bulleted past and Marco barely understood the strange idioms. He was used to the slow turn of language he spoke back home, which was easy because the words rolled from Spanish to English and back, fused into whatever needed to be said; the vocabulary was more invention than distilled convention. He could make up whatever words he wanted so long as they said what needed to be said.

Whether it was in English or Spanish, he rarely spoke to anyone but the johns at the theater. Anyone else would have been a waste of time and a loss of money. He was there to work. He was not like some of the other dancers who came drunk and got high and made idiots of themselves onstage. He supposed it was why Olga, who ran the theater, and who was now headed toward the DJ booth, had called him. She could depend on him.

"Marco," she grumbled, coming up to him with her notepad, "I want you in the duo tonight."

"Who with?" he asked, though it hardly mattered to him. He hated the duo. He had done it a few times, once with Chris and a couple of times with clumsy straight guys. The act was completely unerotic. The dancers went through their individual moves, never really sharing a rhythm of any kind, but the men in the audience sat in rapt attention, as if watching a charade of sex was as satisfying as sex itself. He wondered if Olga ever watched the duo or any of the dancers. Did she know how ridiculous the whole enterprise looked? It was a true burlesque.

Olga flipped through her notepad, dragging her pencil through her gold-streaked hair. The gold highlights made her face look dark and slack. Marco waited for her to tell him the name of his partner, but then, in a defeated flurry, she fanned the pages of the notepad and snapped it shut. She looked up and seemed startled by Marco's face. Had she expected someone else?

She shook her head. "I dunno who it's gonna be," she barked in irritation. "So many of you come late. I dunno who's gonna show tonight. That's why I called you." She turned to the mirrors on the wall and arranged the hair over her forehead. Her face softened, so that she looked a bit more like Esther, who was prettier, younger. "I keep telling them, get here on time, get here on time. I'm gonna start replacing them if they don't come on time." Satisfied with her hair, she turned back to Marco. "I got a long list of guys that want to dance."

Marco nodded, unsure if he should ask her his number in the lineup, though he knew by now that she usually gave him a slot near the end of the show. If she did it because she wanted him to have enough time between dances so that he could make money, or because she lumped all the other skinny boys at the end, he didn't know, and never would. She shook her head in frustration, as if Marco could be blamed for everyone else's failings, and without complaining further, went into the DJ booth. Esther came out of the box office then, the magazine rolled up in her hand.

"Olga tell you about the duo?" she asked.

Marco nodded. "You know my number?"

"You don't have one," she said. "There are too many of you tonight. Olga said you just do the duo."

"I need to dance the whole set," Marco interrupted, thinking with a defensive determination that he would leave the city. "I need the money."

"You'll get what you always get and extra for the duo."

"Are you sure?"

She nodded, patting him on the shoulder, before giving him a slight shove toward the back. He turned around, to ask if Patrick would be working that night, perhaps suggest that they dance together, but Esther had vanished, as if dropped through a trap door.

The theater sat dark and deserted, the seats empty and shut like clams on an abandoned beach. He remembered one night, months ago, when he had come into it almost as empty. He couldn't remember why there were hardly any men there that particular night, but it might have been the late hour, or bad weather. He had been out, getting coffees at Café Le Mirage for Olga, but he now stood in the theater, stopping to see if Chris was still onstage, since he liked to do extravagant numbers with props, but someone else was dancing and Chris was in one of those seats. An old man was whispering into his ear. Marco went closer, hoping he had confused Chris with Tommy, the red head from Little Rock who looked like him. But no, this was Chris, a vulgar pearl tucked between the lips of the seat, and the old man had a wrinkled hand in Chris's pants. With the other hand, the old man pulled out a twenty and Chris stuffed it into his socks. Marco fled to the dressing room. When Chris came around to the lockers where Marco was drinking the coffee he had bought for himself, holding the other bitter cup he had bought Chris, Marco didn't say anything. Chris called him sugar or sweetheart or darling, but the tawdry word, whichever it was, made Marco sick.

Until then, working with Chris the same nights hadn't seemed terrible. They looked so different that they never competed for the same johns, and when they didn't have any work, they went to the arcade and played video games or took photo-booth photos. They also split the cost of a hotel room so that it came out cheaper for both of them. But after seeing Chris with the old man and the short change he went for, Marco never wanted to work the same nights again.

Marco pushed out to the lounge where the punchbowl and the chips and pretzels had been set out for the customers. No one was around here either. He grabbed a plastic cup and filled it with punch, a mix of fruit juices that seemed spiked with alcohol. He was never sure what it had in it, but he could always count on the dull buzz he got toward the middle of the night, and he knew the high was not from dancing or from the money he was making by going out with the men.

He took a drink as the backstage door opened, the light spilling toward him across the carpet, a strange guy standing in near silhouette. Marco had never seen him before. The guy had an uneasy look about him, like he might spit out a knot of garbled words,

51

accented and inflected in all the wrong ways. Marco was sure, even in the dimness, that the guy had a trace of Asian blood: Chinese or Japanese or Vietnamese. The guy had a square jaw and skin as dark and smooth as fired clay. Malaysian?

Marco caught himself—he sounded like the johns who always wanted to figure him out. They always thought he was Filipino or from some uncharted archipelago in the Asian-Pacific Ocean. They never believed he was Mexican. (And nothing else?) They tried to convince him of a tenuous and faint bloodline to the ancient migrants who crossed into the Americas through the Bering Strait. He let them believe what they wanted. He didn't know how to explain his Asian looks anyway. He would nod at whatever fantasy the johns had conjured: his mother was Chinese or Korean or he was the love-child of an American GI who had fought in Vietnam. He lost himself to the peck and pull of their circling desire because it was good for business.

"You coming in?" the guy asked, his voice hard.

Marco nodded, unable to say anything, as if he himself didn't know a recognizable language. He threw away the rest of his punch and passed into the dressing room, moving to an empty locker and arranging his things for the night. He took his time. He hoped the guy was a new dancer. He had to be, since no one else was allowed backstage, though a john once told him about the days when anyone could come back to the dressing room. You didn't have to go to one of the nearby hotels. The going rate for whatever you wanted was much cheaper and you had the added excitement of watching everyone else getting off beside you.

Marco wanted to turn around and see the guy again. Was he even there? He wasn't sure from the quiet that had settled over the room. No sound existed save the steam struggling out of the radiator. Marco wouldn't let himself look, feeling too self-conscious, like being naked in a high school shower room. Besides, soon enough, he reminded himself, he'd see the guy onstage. But then the guy spoke.

"We the only ones here tonight?" he asked.

"They must be out getting food," Marco offered, letting his eyes glance at him, and staring more than he should have, long enough to print the guy's face in his mind. His eyes were dark, as if lined with ink, and they had an obsidian intensity to them, an unknown depth like the beauty mark pooled under the flared nostrils of his nose. His hair came down to his shoulders. The hair attracted Marco most. He guessed it was from not being able to grow out his own hair, which if he even attempted to do, spun in coarse thick curls. He called it his Mexican 'fro. In his family, only he seemed to suffer from it, so he kept his hair cut close.

"What's your name?" Marco asked.

"Jaime."

"Marco."

They shook hands and Marco went back to his locker. He was afraid Jaime was straight by the stiff way in which they shook. He tried not to think about it, hoping his instinct was off balance. At least he wasn't another muscle boy. Jaime was thin and small. He did look Chinese, which surprised Marco because few Asian guys danced at the theater. The only one he knew of was Franklin, a Taiwanese gymnast Chris once dated. Marco spun his combination lock shut and turned back to Jaime.

"Olga tell you to come here this early?" Marco asked.

"Nah, I just wanted to get a feel for the place."

"First time?"

"I've done a few strip contests."

Marco approached him. "But nothing all-out naked?"

"Nah, nothing like that."

"You'll do fine. They'll like you." Someone had said that to him once.

Jaime broke into a crooked smile.

"You hungry?" Marco asked. "There's a noodle shop a few streets down."

"Can we make it back in time? We won't be late?"

"We have an hour until the first show. C'mon, let's go."

"The show starts around six," Marco told Jaime once they were at the restaurant, seated and eating. "The first dancer is always some freak with no neck. He'll strut around the stage, flexing his arms. Boring. Then come the featured dancers. More muscle heads or porn stars. They dance all week. The rest of us come after them. It's like a three-hour stretch from the first dancer to the finale. Then we do the whole show again at nine and midnight."

"What happens in the finale?" Jaime asked.

"You'll love it."

"What happens?"

"We all come out onstage."

"Naked?"

"And with a hard-on, if you can manage it."

"Everyone at once?"

"All twelve. The DJ calls your name and you walk across the stage. The audience claps for their favorite. It's probably the best part of the whole night because it's so stupid. A stage full of naked guys trying to keep their dicks hard."

Jaime didn't say anything, but his eyes were wide and still. Marco thought that this must have been what it was like for Chris, to pass down what you knew to someone who knew nothing. He wasn't sure he liked the responsibility or the suddenly uncomfortable comparison.

"It's not easy," Marco said, and he felt it his duty to say more. "Some nights I can't stand to see another naked body. It's kind of repulsive after a while. Like that meat over there."

He pointed to the hard lacquered slabs hung over the grill. Ducks with their necks twisted, burnt beaks turned into their breasts. Beside them, unfamiliar cavities of ribs and spinal cords stretched like red-glazed lopsided grins. Marco turned back to his plate of curried vegetables and fried dumplings. His food seemed less appetizing.

"Where are you on the line?" Marco asked. "What's your number?"

"Seven. I think she said seven." Jaime smiled. "Lucky number seven."

"It's right in the middle," Marco said. "If you do a private show, being right in the middle means the time between dances gets chopped in half. It leaves you, maybe, an hour and a half to get in and out of your clothes, the theater, and the guy's hotel room."

"How many do you do?"

"What?"

"You know, private shows."

"Have you tried these?" Marco forked one of the last dumplings and bit into it. He dipped the open end into the shallow bowl of soy sauce and then pushed the plate of dumplings away. He hated talking numbers. Everyone always wanted to do better, or at least say they did. "I do about two a night. Some nights one. Some nights three. But four by the end of the weekend. That's my quota."

"How much do you ask for?"

"Have you ever hustled?" Marco wondered if he was going to have to tell Jaime everything. He didn't know if he wanted to take the responsibility and took a swallow of his tea as a way to stall the moment. He looked at Jaime. "Have you ever hustled, like at a bar or anything?"

Jaime shook his head and pushed his food around with his fork.

"One-fifty," Marco said. "That's what everybody asks for."

"And that's where the money is, right? Because she's not paying much."

"You got it. You want the last dumpling?"

"No," he said, putting his fork down.

"You sure? I think I ate more than my share."

"I've had them before. There's a place like this up by Columbia."

"You go to school there," Marco said, sure of himself.

"My girlfriend. She's a grad student."

Marco felt his stomach cramp. He couldn't say he was surprised, but he still felt disappointed. He let the dumpling sit in its plate as Jaime went on about how much his girlfriend said she loved the restaurant. Jaime suspected it was more her fetish for Asian men that made her like it and he purposely ordered a hamburger and fries every time they went.

"So when do you break up with her?" Marco joked.

"Already did," Jaime said with his crooked grin. He looked at Marco for a moment and then forked the remaining dumpling on Marco's plate and shoved it into his mouth. "You know," he said as he chewed, "the food here is better. It's not as greasy. And the inside is nice."

"I like the floor tiles."

"Yeah, I was looking at them. The colors remind me of Mondrian."

"Of what?"

"Mondrian," Jaime said. "He was a painter. He did a lot of paintings with squares. He worked with basic colors like red and yellow and blue. The tiles kind of remind me of that. He did a piece called *Manhattan Jazz* or *Boogie Woogie.* I don't remember, but it looks like that."

"Are you an artist?"

"No, I only know about him from a show at MoMA. I used to work there."

"I'm impressed."

"Don't be. I only took tickets."

Jaime spoke with an even voice, in a pitch that didn't brag or try to mask any fears he might have had. Marco didn't know how Jaime might be with the men, but the dancing alone was enough to scare a lot of new guys off. Even guys who stripped at other places refused to work at the theater once the music started and the idea of stripping to nothing in front of a hundred men hit them like a kick in the crotch. Sitting at the restaurant, Marco didn't think Jaime would make it past the first song. Only the loud-mouthed assholes stayed. Marco himself didn't know why he still danced there. He guessed it was more than money that kept him going back. Chris had been right about that. He could have looked for a regular job, but a "regular job" was that exactly, and it wouldn't do. Dancing at the theater made him feel alive, and talking to Jaime reminded him a little of himself his first night.

"The best thing on the menu used to be a fantastic steamed bun. When you cut into it, it was filled with these thin threads of bread. It looked incredible. They served it with cinnamon sugar and crushed peanuts. They stopped making it a while back. The bread maker went back to China or someplace. Maybe went off to another restaurant, but when he was here, I used to see him pulling the dough, stretching it between his arms, rolling it and then braiding it back into itself and stretching it out again. He kept repeating it until he had this thick cord."

"Sounds intense," Jaime said.

"It was." Marco paused. "That's when I first started working at the theater. When I didn't have a client, I came and ate a loaf of that bread, drank some tea."

"Should we ask for the check?" Jaime laid his napkin on the table. "I don't want to be late."

"You start back. I'll pay."

Jaime pulled out a few bills from his pocket, but Marco told him he would take care of it. He didn't have to say it twice, because Jaime got up and seemed ready to rush out.

"Can I ask you something?" Marco asked.

"Like what?" Jaime's face stiffened with seriousness.

"Forget it." Marco waved him off and dug into his pocket for money.

"No, really, what is it?"

"I'm sorry," Marco said, looking up at him. "I get this question all the time, so I know how it feels, but what are you?"

"What am I?" he repeated, his eyes glancing about the restaurant before settling back on Marco. "I'm a Libra, I think."

Marco laughed. "No, I mean, are you Chinese or Japanese or what?"

"Oh, that. Yeah, I get that a lot," he said. "I'm mixed. My dad is from the Philippines, but my mom, she's just from Pennsylvania. Erie. You?"

"Mexican," Marco said. "And I'm an Aquarius."

Jaime smiled and hurried out, passing in front of the windows, the red neon lettering of the restaurant casting a faint glow over him. Marco was still watching Jaime as the waiter took up their plates and set the bill down with two fortune cookies. His fortune read: *Your reputation is your wealth.*

Back at the theater Marco ran into Victor standing by the exit. It was always the same with all the johns. They would whisper, as Victor did now, how glad they were to see Marco, and then quickly ask if he had a place.

"I could get one," Marco said, not wanting to miss this chance to make the first one-fifty of the night. Now that he wanted to leave the city, the plan clear in his mind, he had to turn as many tricks as he could.

He led Victor through the exit and down the stairs. Olga smiled at him through the window and told him not to forget about the duo. He assured her that he would not and took Victor across the street, passing through the busy drive of the Marriott Marquis Hotel and cutting onto Broadway. Under the night sky, the kinetic neon signs spiraled out into bright whirlpools of light, the Jumbotron television played the news, and the regular theater crowd and the religious fanatics and mimes pushed against one another. Marco and Victor passed dozens of souvenir and camera shops and the Playland arcade. They turned down the street to the Carter Hotel and Marco asked Victor to wait outside while he got a room. According to the sign, the rooms were cheaper than most cab rides, which was funny, but untrue.

For a deteriorating hotel, the lights in the elevator were too bright and determined. The smudged mirrors and the cheap gold-colored accents only multiplied the glare. Marco felt ugly under so much light. He hated looking at himself in that elevator and hated anyone looking at him. He tried to empty his mind by staring at the flashing floor numbers until the doors opened.

The room itself was dark. Victor insisted they leave the lights off and walked to the bathroom. He turned on the light over the sink and left the bathroom door open a crack on his way back. A sliver of light came into the room like a beam from the moon. Victor moved to the bed and removed his clothes. Marco hung his coat on the back of a chair and laid his folded shirt and jeans on a polished table that seemed to belong to another hotel. The gold-framed mirror hanging over the table also seemed out of place. But in the dimness, Marco was able to look at himself in the mirror. He thought he looked better in it. He was glad they had left the room dark.

The bed was huge. It made even Victor, a man in his forties who once played football for a college in Jersey, look small. Sitting there in his underwear, his skin was loose and pale and damp with sweat from the walk. Marco came up to him and Victor slid his hands inside his underwear, ran them along the waistband and then quickly pulled them down. Marco's dick flopped out and Victor put it into his mouth as if it might escape him. He sucked a little too hard, but it felt good, and felt better when Victor pulled on Marco's hips to get him deeper into his throat. Marco arched and thrust himself in until he felt Victor's throat give.

Victor sat unmoving. He seemed to have suffered a moment of paralysis, as if he might slump to his side and never rise again, but then he slowly removed his mouth, trailing a line of spit. He ran his hands over Marco's chest, pinching his nipples, sucking them hard. Again, it was too much. Marco complained when Victor slid his tongue into his armpits.

"It's sensitive," he said, and jerked away.

"I know," Victor said with an adolescent glee.

He slid his tongue in again even as Marco forced his arm flat against his side. Getting his armpits eaten felt too good, and he didn't want Victor doing that to him, didn't want Victor to know how turned on he felt.

Marco reached for Victor's dick, but Victor pushed his hands away which was fine with him. He preferred doing nothing. He stood between Victor's legs as Victor slid his hands over Marco's ass, running a finger up his crack. He wanted to finger-fuck. He always tried. He massaged Marco's asshole with his finger, but Marco squeezed tight so that Victor wouldn't be able to push through.

"Victor?"

"Yeah, I know. I just thought maybe." His voice faded to a flat tone that still kept a faint ring of hope. "Here, you lie down. I want to service you. I want to service you so bad. You want to be serviced?"

Marco said yes only to shut him up. Serviced. He hated the word. It made him feel like his father's El Camino.

Victor ran his tongue over Marco's balls and up the shaft of his dick. Marco was hard, but bored. How many times could he get sucked and find it interesting? He sat up and watched Victor's tongue pushing his balls up one at a time. Victor swallowed one and then the other and then he let them pop out from his mouth.

He lifted Marco's hips to get under him, his tongue sliding into Marco's asshole. He ran his tongue around the outside and then plunged it in deep. Marco was ready to come. He grabbed his own dick and began to stroke himself. He moaned for Victor, so that he would know he was ready to pop, and get out of there, but it felt good to moan. It rippled out from the small of his back, traveling deep within the ridge of his spine, up and around the cage of his ribs.

Marco spread his legs wide so that Victor could eat the rest of his ass. Victor's dick was hard and Marco put it into his mouth. He did it without thinking, or rather, he did it as he was thinking of Jaime, not thinking about Victor at all. He hardly sucked a john's dick anymore. Not since finding out he could get away with not doing it and still get paid the same money. But that night he felt good. He was enjoying himself, letting himself enjoy himself, and he would have taken anything in his mouth. He licked Victor's nearly hairless balls and the soft flabby inside of his thighs. Victor moaned. Marco spit into his palm and started pulling on Victor's dick.

At once, which made him wonder why he never noticed it before, he felt the small bump near the head of Victor's dick. Marco slowed his pace. Victor continued to moan. The tongue in Marco's ass went cold. He loosened the hold he had on Victor's dick, but left the pad of one finger on the bump. He felt it, rubbed it, as if he might guess its mystery by touch. He looked at Victor's dick in the dim light, but could not see a thing, which had been the point, he guessed. Victor came in watery squirts, staining the bedcovers, and Marco rolled off the bed and shut himself in the bathroom.

"Are you okay in there?" Victor said through the door.

He said it in a way that made Marco think he'd had a good time. He imagined Victor with a stupid smile on his face. Marco couldn't answer, his mouth open wide, looking through the mirror at his teeth and tongue and the inside of his cheeks. He didn't know what he expected to see. He spat into the sink and rinsed his mouth out with hot water.

"Marco, you okay?" Victor sounded concerned. He knocked on the door. "Should I come in there?"

"No," Marco shot out. "I'm fine. Just washing up."

"You can't be late for your number."

"I know. I'll be right out."

Marco spit into the toilet and flushed.

What would have been the point of saying anything? It was over and he had the money stuffed into his coat pocket. The wad of bills pressed against Jaime's fortune cookie. He was careful not to crush the cookie as he ran back to the theater. Olga was laughing with a blond woman in the box office. He wondered if it was Madonna, who was rumored to know them, to come in every once in a while to catch the show. He used to fantasize that she would see him one night and save him somehow. It wasn't her though, it was some other woman he didn't know, but Olga seemed to be in a good mood which meant he wasn't late.

She slipped him the key and told him he would be dancing with a guy named Romeo. Was she joking? Or was the guy? Romeo? The name was worse than those he'd heard before, names like Austin or Taylor or Laredo. With the name of any city on a Texas map, a guy could find work as a stripper.

Marco shot into the booth. "Manuel, is this Romeo for real?"

"Shh," Manuel snapped, not bothering to pull his face from where he had it jammed into the window. "He's out there dancing."

Marco went to Manuel. The Madonna record spun on the turntable, playing the song he had listened to earlier, the one that should have been his, a tune about angels and saints. He liked it now despite its almost obvious and pained lyrics. Manuel scooted over on his stool and Marco looked out onto the stage.

The guy was naked. He must have been on his second song. He couldn't dance. He seemed to walk about the stage without even the barest hint of a rhythm. At least he had a good-sized dick, Marco thought. The balls were a bit loose, nearly withered, and he had too much pubic hair, but the rest of him seemed better than average. His dark and luminescent skin bounced back the light where sweat had collected. Marco got a better look at the guy as he pushed his sticky hair back and his surprise nearly sent him stumbling against the turntable. It was Jaime. Marco had not recognized him without his clothes. For better or worse, no one ever looked the same naked.

"Let's hear it for Romeo," Manuel moaned into the microphone. He turned out the lights and cued the next song. He glanced at Marco and sighed. *"No tan mal,* but she couldn't get it up. *Asi es la vaina."*

"It's his first time," Marco defended, though he didn't know why. It should have been good news. Supposedly, only the gay boys suffered from stage fright.

"No chama, those straight boys come out, *coño,* rock hard. *Salen con el palo duro duro duro. Hasta á mi se me para la vaina. Imaginate."*

"They're trash."

"Aye, no importa. They're hard and that's all that matters. Ask any of the *tíos* out there." Manuel laughed, his eyes fluttering like a man in the midst of a miracle healing.

Backstage Jaime stood naked and with the kind of lazy insolence that had always irritated Marco. He probably even slept naked in winter, Marco thought, which Marco never did in any season, another of Chris's complaints. Except for one or two other guys sitting around, flipping through porn magazines, the dressing room was empty, which meant business was good.

"You forgot this, *Romeo,"* Marco said, pulling out the fortune cookie.

"It's my brother's name."

"Sure," Marco teased. "Here. Take it." He held the cookie out to him.

"I don't believe in fortunes," Jaime said, moving to his locker.

"Oh, c'mon. You don't want to know what it says?"

"The last time I got one, the paper was blank."

"So they fell asleep at the fortune cookie plant. You know they make them in Brooklyn?"

"No thanks," he said, moving to his locker.

Marco looked at the cookie and cracked it open and read its fortune. He stuffed the scrap into his jeans and wondered if it was bad luck to open two fortune cookies, whether one canceled out the other. He should have left it at the restaurant. He felt like an idiot for having brought it.

"So, what did it say?" Jaime asked.

"What does it matter? You don't believe in it." Marco ate the cookie, the hard almond-flavored communion of hope dissolving in his mouth. "And put your clothes back on. The duo is coming up."

"So it's you and me?"

"Yeah," Marco said, unsure what he heard behind Jaime's voice. "You got a problem with it? I can get someone else."

"No. I was hoping it was you. I haven't really talked to anyone else." He leaned toward Marco at his locker. "We're not going to fuck out there, are we?"

"Not if you don't want to," Marco said, but when Jaime staggered backward, he caught him by the arm and added that he was only kidding. "It's like sex, only none of it is real." Marco hated the sound of this even as he said it. He wanted it to be real.

Marco sat alone on the edge of the stage ramp and waited for the start of the song. Manuel had picked it out. He had guaranteed it would be something different and not another track from the new Madonna album he had been playing all night.

The microphone popped over the speakers and Manuel poured out a breathy introduction. The music trumpeted the sound of maracas and the roll of hand-slapped congas. Manuel has got to be kidding, thought Marco, and he shot a look toward the dim booth. Manuel waved like a kid pressed against the back windshield of a car receding into the distance. Surprised by the music, Marco was unsure how to dance to the tropical beats. They were not at all like the rhythms he danced with his mother, the music played by father's band. This sound had a muscular feel to it, and was less sentimental than those Mexican songs his father played. Whoever this was, and whatever it was they were playing, he began to take it in and let move through his body. The beats came quick, and Marco was grateful that Manuel hadn't played a sappy love song. He winked at Manuel in the booth and then looked out over the audience. The men in front must have thought he winked at them because they smiled back with all their teeth showing, though some had gaps where teeth were missing.

He pulled his shirt off, rubbing it over his chest, slinging it over his shoulder as if to dull the sharp heat from an imagined Carribean sun. At any moment, he expected the men to shift in their seats, their eyes darting from him to a point behind him. That would be Jaime coming out onstage. Marco had told him to strut around, as if lost, and then come over. He would lead them from there.

The song continued its rhythm, racheting along until a male voice dropped in amid the instruments and began singing about a girl whom he wanted but was too afraid to approach. Marco should have felt Jaime's hands by then. He turned around to see if he was onstage at all. He was, but in the darkest area, pressed against the glittering back curtain. He stood unmoving, like some kid at his first high school dance, frozen by the fear of rejection. Great, Marco thought, pushing himself to his feet. He should have known better than to agree to this duet.

He approached Jaime, taking his steps slow, glancing up at him every few steps. He was afraid Jaime would rush out between the curtains, but Jaime stayed put, perhaps too frightened to do anything more than stand as Marco circled him one way, and then the other. Marco grabbed Jaime's hands and dragged him down the stage to the front end of the ramp. The music climbed up and down an intricate ladder of chords. And as if taking his cue from the sudden note that blared into a single high pitch and then dropped down into a heavy wave of beats, Marco began unbuttoning Jaime's shirt and unbuckling his belt, pulling it off. The men in the audience leaned forward with anticipation.

The song kept going. It seemed to have no end, repeating itself with stinging Spanish words, the effect intoxicating Marco like tequila poured down his throat. He came up behind Jaime and slipped the belt around his neck. Marco ground his hips into him and yanked his head back, hoping to find a terrified, humiliated look on his face. This was what Marco wanted, he suddenly realized, to embarrass this straight guy in front of all the men watching and the other dancers lined up against the wall. He didn't expect Jaime to kiss him. He didn't expect Jaime's hungry mouth to clamp down on his.

Marco loosened the belt around Jaime's neck and began pulling off his own clothes, not for the men (there were no other men as far as he could see in his feverish state), but for Jaime on this imaginary beach. Jaime seemed to wake to this moment, to this vision Marco had stoked for them, and he touched Marco now, his hands warm and tender, so unlike the men now lost to the sea. Marco wanted this moment to last, like the singer now sang, like his body seemed to sing. He and Jaime were naked, their jeans puddled around their feet, underwear swimming in the soft denim. Marco felt the pull of reality. It tugged at him and threatened to take them both. Marco tried to put it out of his mind, matching Jaime in movement, pressing his body against him. Together they rocked.

Jaime, who had been following Marco's lead, suddenly pulled back and knelt against the stage floor. The men in the audience shifted in their seats, the crescendo of creaks drowning out the music and washing away the moment. One man gasped, ohmigod. The theater came tumbling back, Marco standing at the end of the stage, Jaime pressing his face into his crotch, stroking him, ready to take him into his mouth. Marco panicked. He didn't know how far they could go, what the rules were, the law. Even with Chris, their routine was just that, a rehearsed dance of empty movements.

He pushed Jaime against the dirty stage floor and began the canned coreography he used to do with Chris, but already the lights were dimming, the music receding like a tide. Manuel's voice came up, high-pitched and nervous: "Let's hear it for the Dynamic Duo . . . " For the first time, Manuel didn't have his breathy sex voice.

The lights out, and the dance over, Marco helped Jaime up from the stage floor. Jaime grabbed his clothes, dusted himself off, and then whispered, hot against Marco's ear, that he shouldn't have stopped the show. He dove back behind the curtain before Marco could said anything. When he found his pants, Marco glanced out into the audience and saw a field of glimmering old eyes, the drowned men had become a kaleidoscope of faded stars.

It was quiet backstage. None of the guys said anything to each other. Even the muscle guys flipped through their porn magazines without saying a word. Marco didn't know if it had been his act onstage that had silenced them or if they were concentrating for the finale.

When the last dancer came off the stage, the house lights came up, and Manuel called back the dancers in his sex voice again. As usual everyone refused to be the first one out under the bright house lights. Manuel came hurtling through the dressing room, hollering for everyone to get out there, clapping his hands to get the guys moving, slapping a few bare asses.

"*Aye puta*," Manuel gasped, catching Marco. "You were too much. I think *la* Olga got a little mad. You know how she is about real sex. *Una ladilla esa vieja. Que se jode.*"

Back in his booth, Manuel again called the dancers to the stage. Jaime had disappeared in the blur of bodies and Marco found himself standing among the freaks, feeling small, alone. When they called Jaime, he strutted out as if his dick dragged the floor. On the walk back he stood beside Marco but Marco pretended not to notice.

Manuel called Marco to take a bow by himself, which surprised him since he hadn't danced a solo. He took his bow, though, and returned to Jaime's side. The last guy, who had drank too much punch to settle his nerves, tripped and fell from the stage, detonating an explosion of laughs throughout the theater. He picked himself up, but refused to stay for the next two shows. Olga put Marco in the guy's slot, and without an explanation, canceled the duo.

For the second and third show, Manuel let Marco have his song, a reward for making a *desmadre*, an entertaining disaster, as he called it, of the duo. Olga and Esther said nothing to Marco all night. He hoped he was still going to get the money they had promised him. He really needed it now that he was going to sit out the rest of the night, not wanting to go out with any of the other johns because of what had happened with Victor. Marco was still shaken by the discovery of the bump, going to the bathroom every few minutes to spit. He kept passing Jaime back-stage, then saw him in the lounge where he sat eating pretzels and talking to a few johns, the weekend regulars. He tried to get Jaime's attention, to tell him those men never had money, but when he realized what he was doing, that he was becoming pro-tective and obsessive about a straight guy, he decided to go to the Playland arcade.

Playland was a gritty, smoke-filled maze of weathered video games and roughneck kids who, like Marco that night, had nowhere else to go and nothing better to do. Men sometimes hurried in and left with a kid or two, but Marco never got picked up there. He guessed he was too old, at least under those lights, to pull off the underage look. He dropped a few quarters into the video games and lost quickly. Whatever skill he'd had as a kid was now gone.

From the arcade, Marco crossed Broadway to a fast-food joint overlooking Times Square. He gulped down a milkshake and began to think that Jaime might help bust the lock Chris seemed to have on him, but then Marco worried that he would be getting out of one trap only to land in another. He wasn't supposed to get involved with anyone, not with another working guy, and even less with an admitted straight one, that was what he had told him-self after the last breakup with Chris. The personal rule was sup-posed to keep him sane in this business of retail sex. Some nights, as he darted through an unfamiliar street to a john's apartment, or as he masturbated to sleep, alone in his bedroom, Marco thought he would wait to find a boyfriend until the moment was right, though he wasn't sure when that would be, waiting was just what he was used to.

He had spent most of his life waiting: to get out of the *colonia* in which he lived, for his heart to warm to Chris, for the johns to come to him, or the nights to end, whichever came first. His moth-er had taught him all about waiting the hours she sat at the dance halls, in search of a man who might dance with her, and then, when the band played its last song, and the band brokeup, for Marco's father to get sober. His mother would pile him and the rest of them into the car and drive to the new San Juan shrine.

(The old one had burned to the ground when a prop plane crashed into it. His mother claimed the pilot kamikazed into it and was later found impaled on a crucifix.) At the shrine, Marco filled rinsed-out gallon milk jugs with holy water from the blessed taps and read the *promesas* and scanned the wallet photos and mementos left in one of the chambers. He always hoped to find someone he knew, a neighbor, or a fellow student at school. He would also help his mother light a candle. It was a *milagro,* she would say, that the new shrine didn't burn down from the heat of the flickering sea of candles. She would make them kiss the wounded feet of Jesus on the way out and then return home to wait for whatever miracles she had petitioned *la Virgencita* and the other saints.

Back at the theater Marco performed his final solo dance for the night and then went to his locker. Backstage felt like a steam room. The air was hot and wet from the radiators and sweating bodies and his skin felt singed by the heat. At his locker, drinking from his water bottle, he nearly choked when Jaime tapped him on the shoulder. Jaime was wearing a pair of boxers and nothing else. Marco had not put on any clothes since coming off the stage either. It would have been a wasted effort since the last finale of the night was next.

"Did you get a place?" Marco asked, passing Jaime the water.

Jaime shook his head. "I haven't been out," he said, taking a swallow. "What's with that anyway? Am I ugly?"

"It's like that the first night," Marco said, wanting another drink, wanting to put his mouth where Jaime's had been. "I don't think I had any business my first night either. You come back tomorrow and I'm sure you'll just sweep this place out. I don't remember my first night at all, so it must not have been very good." Marco didn't know why he was being nice. Most guys bragged that the demand forced the johns to take numbers.

Manuel came through, clapping his hands.

"You two," he shouted at Marco and Jaime. "Get your little buns out on stage. It's the finale and *la* Olga is going to give me a *coñataso* if you don't go out there. *¡Orale! ¡Muevense!*"

68

Marco half-ignored him and turned back to Jaime. "If you need a place, I got room 626 at the Carter. It's a dump, but it's a place to crash for the night. I think the television works."

He hoped Jaime didn't think it was a pickup. Or, he hoped Jaime was smart enough to realize it was, but wouldn't freak out about it. Marco wanted to have sex with him, which surprised him because he never wanted to have sex with anybody after a show.

Instead of the usual greasy fatigue he felt at the end of the night, Marco felt a bit disoriented and horny. No one else rushed to get their clothes on and leave the theater either. No one seemed to have anyplace to go. Even the guys who went to the female strip joints hung back.

Marco's eyes burned as he emptied his locker. He needed to take out his contacts and put on his glasses, but he waited to see if Jaime was going back to the hotel with him. If he was coming along, Marco would leave the contacts in, never mind the burning, because glasses were as bad for love as they were for business. He knew he could be giving his ass away for free and no one would want it if he wore glasses. He pretended to still be busy with his clothes and things as Jaime prepared to leave. Then he was gone. Not a word of good-bye.

Marco faced his locker, his body stiff with rejection. He felt like one of those celebrity cardboard cutouts propped in tourist shop windows. From their flat necks hung pathetic signs crying: *BUY ME! TAKE ME HOME!*

He hung back a few more minutes, taking out his contacts, slipping on his glasses before leaving the theater. He didn't find Jaime at the bottom of the stairs or at the corner by the Howard Johnson as he hoped he would. He began to walk back to the hotel, his disappointment draped over him like a heavy coat. Everything was closed and shut down. The Jumbotron hung blind over Times Square. A single white dot floated in the black frame. The electronic news zipper underneath was likewise blank. Playland sat dumb and mute. The street-level billboard, an art project that read EVERYBODY in large black letters, looked as if it were being pulled down. The chairs bolted into the bright yellow billboard, chairs in which tourists sometimes sat for pictures and a few crazies sat to read the paper, were smashed or crumbling.

Marco passed the side street for the hotel without knowing it and found himself on Forty-second. He decided to take the long way back, stopping at the 24-hour luncheonette for a hot dog. All he had to look forward to was sleep anyway. Halfway up the street of all-night movie houses and porn shops, three kids in huge jackets stopped as Marco came up to them. They got into crouched stances, as if ready to leap into the air with a few karate kicks they might have seen done by Bruce Lee. One of them shrieked in mock Chinese. His breath burst from his mouth like a fire-eater spouting flames into the night.

Marco almost laughed. The johns weren't the only ones who thought he was Chinese. He didn't understand it. Still, the confusion gave him a frustrated pleasure, and he was ready to say something until he spotted the kid with the serious and determined eyes and Marco knew this one kid was going to hit him. This particular kid didn't seem at all entertained by what his friends were doing. He just stood there, in the middle of the sidewalk, wearing a jacket the color of pale sunshine. They had more than enough room on that sidewalk at that hour to walk around each other, but Marco didn't want them to think he was afraid. He had never felt afraid in Times Square because he felt he belonged. Other nights he felt invisible. Tonight, the hour simmering with the promise of morning, Marco pushed past the kid and headed for the luncheonette. The kid knocked Marco across the side of the face before he got to the door.

Marco staggered a few steps, stunned from the explosion of pain and light and the sudden absence of sound. He bent over and everything swelled and shut. He kept feeling a sloughing off of matter inside his ear, as if his eardrum had ruptured or had been pressed into blood like grapes smashed into wine. He couldn't move at all and only stood there, bent over the sidewalk, looking down into the concrete where his glasses had been flung. The glasses weren't his. Chris had given him this pair when his got broken. That had been in Houston, when they still wore the same prescription. Had he smashed them at the running track?

He wasn't sure. And he wasn't sure now how long he stood there, looking at these glasses that were now his.

The kid who had hit him ran off, though he was unsure of that too. He might have walked away, for all Marco knew. He felt too disoriented to react. The other two kids laughed and taunted him. They were too young for Marco to bother with, but humiliation flared in his gut and threatened to take him in its fire. He gathered his glasses and what dignity he had left and straightened himself to stumble toward the luncheonette.

He didn't put his glasses back on because he figured if he couldn't see anyone, no one could see him, but there was no one in the luncheonette other than the cook. A radio blared from behind the counter. The cook asked Marco what he was going to have and pointed to the caricatures of food painted on the walls. Marco wondered if the cook had seen what had happened but was deciding to ignore it, not caring if he was hurt.

Marco didn't want to eat, but he ordered a hot dog to keep from getting thrown out (in New York it was always buy something or leave), and as he reached for his money, his hands went cold and shook. Had the kids run off with his one-fifty? Or had he dropped it in the fight? Would anyone have called it a fight? He chased out his monkey thoughts and felt for the wad in his sock, and reassured, left it. He paid for his hotdog with the small bills in his pocket and sat at the counter.

The two kids appeared at the window. They burst out laughing. The cook waved his spatula at them and the feeble threat made them laugh even harder. They fell onto the sidewalk, kicking and pounding the concrete until it seemed to crack open and swallow them up. Marco couldn't eat. His jaw hurt too much. But he didn't want to leave. He needed the safety of the cook and his spatula. Marco stared at his hot dog until the music pulsed too loud against his ears and the lights felt like hot lamps. He asked for a bag to take his food and then stepped outside, looking up and down the sidewalk, and then across to the other side of the street. He didn't want to be afraid, but with each step toward the hotel, he kept turning behind him to see if the kids were coming out of the shadows to bust the rest of his face.

Marco dropped the hot dog into a trash can as he passed a trannie bar and entered the hotel. The lobby felt crummier than usual. The threadbare couches seemed more worn and without color. The anemic palms shriveled in their pots. The Korean woman didn't even bother to ask Marco for his key, as she usually did at that hour, but maybe she saw he was hurt.

The hard lights in the elevator forced his eyes shut. He didn't want to look at himself in the glass, not even to check if his ear was swelling, if it was there at all. He heard the ping of the passing floors and decided that when he got to his room he would go right to sleep. He would feel better in the morning.

When he stepped out of the elevator and turned down the hall, he caught sight of Jaime at his door, drinking a cup of coffee. If Jaime hadn't spotted him at the same moment, Marco might have rushed back to the elevators. He didn't want Jaime now. Not like this.

"What took so long?" Jaime asked, leaning against the dingy wallpaper.

"I had to get something to eat," Marco said, approaching with his head down, jaw aching with each step.

"I ate too," Jaime grunted. "But I didn't take no thirty minutes."

Marco wanted to smile, if only to be polite, but the thought of it made his jaw hurt. He kept his face down, and with his stiffened fingers unlocked the door and let them both into the dark room.

Their clothes fell away like the cold outside. They stood in front of the bed, Marco unmoving, Jaime starting to kiss his neck, behind his ears. A sudden flash washed out the room in a hurricane of bright pain churning out from Marco's ear. Another kiss and another flash and Marco began a clinical, systematic inventory of the pain shooting through his body, the parts afflicted, the intensity of their suffering.

Jaime kissed him again, lips across jaw, tongue in ear. Marco jerked away, and stood there, stalled in his desire. Jaime, his breath heavy against Marco's face, smelled of coffee and pulled Marco in and out of consciousness. Marco felt himself against an unseen stretch of ropes, an imagined crowd screaming a count slowly winding down. He was going to lose. He was going down a loser.

He thought if he could just drag his tongue along the inside of Jaime's thigh, the night could still be saved, but the pain lit over the horizon again, breaking like an unpleasant morning. He felt the walls falling away, the bed plunging the six floors down to the street, and he drifted in the space where the room had been, suspended as if inside Jaime's velvet mouth.

Marco didn't want to cry, but when he asked, could they just stop, he felt a sharp pain in his body, a delayed tremor from the blow. Who had hit him? Why? Why couldn't he come up and lie over Jaime, this guy he'd wanted all night? He imagined them fused together, nipples and cocks and legs pressed against each other, their bodies held together as if the other might escape, as if they could not hold enough.

"What's wrong?" Jaime asked, letting go of Marco's hand. They had been holding hands since they stepped into the room, but Marco only now realized it as Jaime let go. Marco reached out, stiff with pain, but his hands grabbed at nothing but the warm air.

He tried to say nothing was wrong, everything was fine and he was fine, but not even a whisper escaped his mouth. His lips trembled from the effort and he felt the room going white again. Jaime stood in front of him, bleached out from the light, his eyes diluted to pools of creamed coffee drying in abandoned spoons. It was the way those eyes looked back, cool and evaporating into a dry disappointment, that Marco felt his chest give, the ribs snapping and collapsing into the smoldering heap of his heart. He felt impaled by the sharp cry of his breaking body.

winter

f●ur

Marco was hoping to sidestep the puddle by taking the muddy rim banking the track, but when he looked up, a woman was headed toward the same thin pass. He pushed himself faster to beat her to it. She seemed altogether oblivious to him. He had the urge to shout that she was going the wrong way (all the signs on the fence pointed runners in the other direction—the direction he was running—to avoid situations like this), but instead of making a scene, he tucked his chin against his chest, letting his scarf ride over his mouth, and leaped over the puddle. His heel made a faint splash as it came down hard on the other side. He didn't care so much about getting wet. It was his stride he didn't want to break. If he stopped, he went cold like the puddles that riddled the track. He liked to run past the puddles instead of hurtling over them because then he could look into their silvery reflection of the world, as if it were an opening to another, making him doubt the authenticity of the one in which he ran. On sullen mornings, when his muscles felt tight, his joints unhinged, and mood troubled, he feared splashing through to the other side, resurfacing into a puddle on the road of his old *colonia*.

This morning the sky had the color of dingy blankets, the cold weather treasures the homeless pulled out of the garbage, damp and unraveling. The air felt sharp, as if it cleaved into every part of him, scraping him clean inside. He was running for the air, hoping to calm himself, become something like the reservoir, dark and patient. He had been doing well, staying away from Chris, seeing a couple of regulars. He had not let himself get stupid over Jaime. He let Jaime call first. Never mind that the call came two weeks after their night at the hotel. That he called at all was enough, since Marco had not bet on anything going on past that first night.

The few times he had hoped to see a dancer from the theater, and Patrick had been one, at first, Marco had come away disappointed. He had to get used to the fuck-and-run sex of guys who never slowed down enough after the orgasm to exchange names, much less a phone number, even a fake one. Everyone seemed in a headlong rush to smash their body against another. Sex was like that, quick and brutal, leaving Marco bruised in too many places. He had expected the same from Jaime, considering that he was straight, and that most new dancers rarely returned a second time.

At the hotel, the moment he had started crying, Marco thought he'd hear the door slam, the receding steps of Jaime rushing to the elevators. But he stayed. He didn't even ask for sex. They lay together, and in Jaime's arms, Marco spoke about the fight with the kids, claiming all three had jumped him so that Jaime wouldn't think he was a *vieja* for not being able to defend himself. *Vieja* would have been something Marco's father might have said, refusing to ask him if he was all right, stinging his wounds with *Sangre de Chango*, the only comfort he might have offered. The night with Jaime, however, felt so tender. They awoke in each other's arms the following morning and made love. That was what it was to Marco. Since moving to New York, he hadn't met anyone who was as generous as Jaime, who seemed to get pleasure in giving it, who held him until the sweat and cum had dried against their skin.

The following night, Jaime was back at the theater, and before the start of the first show asked Marco if he could borrow the hotel room. He had his first john. Dancers rented out their rooms if they weren't using them, always for a fee, but Marco let Jaime have it for nothing. His first impulse was to follow Jaime to the hotel to make sure he would be all right. He had nothing else to do before his next dance anyway, but he decided against it, and stayed in the lounge, sitting out another night, taking a few numbers for later in the week. He massaged his still aching jaw and the bruise behind his ear which had bloomed like an exotic flower. Jaime went out with his john between dances and returned without incident. Other johns circled him, but none took him out, and so Jaime and Marco spent the rest of their hours together. At the end of the night, as Marco readied to leave, Jaime lingered next to him, a grave expression on his face, the same inky seriousness of the presidents on the cash Olga gave them on their way out.

Without even discussing it, Jaime spent that night with Marco too. Marco tried not to make more of it. He had to brace himself for the disappointment to come. He was certain Jaime would disappear early the next morning, but again, he remained and persuaded Marco to follow him to his downtown apartment where they made love again on a waterbed, the kind that didn't make a person sick. They parted with the promise to see each other soon. Marco began to think it was a possibility, but as the days passed without so much as a phone call, days that grew dark and muted as the photo-booth photos they had taken at the arcade, Marco began heading to the running track, determined to wring out the damp hopes clogging his lungs. He ran for miles. He ran in cold and rain and biting back pain.

When Jaime called, he said they should hang out some night. There were no explanations about being out of town, or having misplaced the number, nothing to redeem the wait Marco had suffered, nothing even so much as a lie, just this vague invitation to go out. Marco forgave him, at least in his mind, and suggested they go to a midtown dance club. The memory of their two nights still swilled in his head, strong and dumbing as a double shot of tequila. Drunk on his fantasy, he could hear the music clawing and scratching at the air: deep bass, drum beats, electronic synthetic chords, an incoherent vocabulary of words spliced and repeated, everything twisting in on itself like a lyrical sea of drowned musicians.

Jaime said, no, not tonight, maybe another time because he was really calling for the address of a hustler bar he had heard about. Marco bobbed up from his chimerical sea, eyes stung and throat raw, his desire wrecked with doubt. Jaime didn't want him enough. He guessed that for Jaime, like for so many others he knew, guys were a quick way to get off. After a furtive encounter, they could go home to their dinners and get on with their lives. Jaime didn't have the immolating passions that Chris had, however false those flames had been, however quick to die.

After that wounding phone call, the days passed like night, slow and dark, with a tincture of sadness. A bitter cold clamped down on the city. Fierce gusts rifled through garbage cans and pushed the world without direction. Marco continued his runs to keep himself moving, his thoughts from turning to Jaime, but then his knee began to ache. He bought a new pair of running shoes, and on the way out of the shoe store, another idea sprinted into his head. His mother, he remembered, had once cast a spell to help *las cuatas* clinch the guys they liked. He rushed to a stationery store and bought a sheet of expensive paper speckled with rose petals. When he got home, he cut out two strips, wrote Jaime's name on them and stuffed them into his new shoes. Out on the track, he invoked Jaime with each pounding step.

He had the paper in his shoe now as he came to the end of the lap. He'd only planned to do one, since his knee still ached, but with the sudden memory of Jaime, as if his voice shot through the air and rushed about his ears, he decided to go for another. He would slog through the miles until Jaime called with a definite invitation to dinner or a movie.

He passed the bridge that led back home and quickened his stride, leaving behind the runners he had kept pace with, letting the bare trees and shrubs blur into a muted discoloration. He felt recharged, nearly free and filled with possibility. The sun might appear and burn away the gray. Anything could happen.

As he came onto the turn in the track he felt himself stagger forward, as if suffering from a cramp, the pain shooting up through his right hip. He pressed forward, passing the stone building that banked the reservoir, a structure that housed an antiquated pump. If he pushed on, he thought to himself, the pain might just work itself out. It had gone away all the other times. He tried to shake his legs out, exaggerating his stride, though the effort only brought down more weight onto his legs. The right knee felt disjointed. He decided to keep his pace until he reached the steps that led down to Fifth Avenue, where he would stretch and walk the rest of the lap, but before he could give it another thought, he felt his knee give, as if a rock had been slammed against it. He jerked forward and stopped short of falling into the mud. A few runners sprinted past and he stood watching them.

He limped home and put himself into a warm bath. He set the knee with a pack of ice and then rubbed in an ointment. His mother had once admitted it was for injured horses, but swore to it the mornings she woke up after a night of too much dancing in heels. He thought he would feel instant relief, but the ointment did nothing more than make his knee feel greasy. He tried another folk remedy, this one with an egg plucked raw from the fridge. He brushed the egg over his knee and visualized the pain being soaked up by the yolk through the shell and then broke the egg into a glass of water and let it stand overnight by the bed. The knee didn't improve by morning, and in his mounting desperation, he felt guilty for having put those scraps of paper into his shoe. If he had not insisted on forcing Jaime under his spell, he wouldn't be suffering the pain afflicting him now. He considered throwing the scraps out, shrugging it off as *brujeria*, as he always had, as his father had, until Jaime called a second time.

five

When Marco limped into the bar, John came up to him, took his hand, and led him to a dark corner. A cranberry soda already waited for him. Fine, Marco thought, he would drink the soda and then wander to the back to see if Jaime was here. That was why he was here, to see Jaime, not to turn a trick, and especially not to meet up with John. John had made an ass of himself the last time. He had drunk so much he couldn't read the street signs on the cab ride home and had made Marco shout them out only to congratulate him later for being literate. Tonight, John seemed sober, and he stood pressed against Marco, blocking him from the rest of the bar. Marco couldn't see past John's thinning gray hair, his bright red sweater and the bleached bone he claimed to have found in the Chihuahua desert. It hung from his neck like a dog tag. Marco was supposed to be impressed or flattered because his parents came from Mexico and John had guessed it immediately. None of the other johns ever had.

"I was hoping you'd be here," John said, sipping a glass of wine.

"You have plans for me?" Marco asked.

"You want me to be brutal?"

"You want *me* to be brutal," Marco said, trying to make a joke.

"No," John gushed, a simpering heat flickering across his face. "Do you want me to be brutal? You know, honest, about what I want?"

Marco shrugged and took a swallow of his drink.

"Well," John said, hushing a bit and becoming serious, "I want you to come home with me tonight. To Brooklyn."

Marco nodded.

"And I want you to stay a bit longer."

"I stayed the full hour last time."

"Yes, I know," John countered, his voice fading to a nervous apology. "But you see, it's just that, well, there we were, and then zippo. You left."

"But it was an hour," Marco protested. "Maybe even an hour and a half."

"I know." John laughed softly. "I just need more time. I need to stretch out and relax."

"How much time do you need?"

"Well, I'd love for you to stay forever." John paused, taking a sip of his wine, his eyes never leaving Marco. "But at least, you know, overnight."

Marco shifted his weight, hoping to slip out from the corner he felt backed into. He wanted to search the rest of the dim bar for Jaime. A couple of guys in jeans and leather jackets sat in the back watching the television that hung from the rafters. Jaime wasn't among them. An electronic message strip announced: *Le Beaujoulais Nouveau est arrivé*, and then, *ANYONE Caught Soliciting Will Be Thrown OUT.* Marco always found both messages a joke.

He checked his watch. It was after nine. In an hour or two, the place would fill. He hated the bar then, waiting around for a pick-up, refusing to work the johns like the other guys, who made the rounds clutching their bottled beers like their dicks, babbling to anyone who listened about how much they had made last week or last month. Three, five, seven hundred dollars a night, they'd say. Tax-free. When Marco had told Jaime about the scene, Jaime had said he hated the sound of it too. Marco liked that. He thought perhaps they both still had some self-respect.

"I know we had a previous arrangement," John said, pulling Marco out of his thoughts. "But I think it's just too high."

"What? The price?"

"Well, yes."

Marco looked around, ready to walk off and join the other guys in the back. They might be loud-mouthed hustlers, but he preferred their company over having to bargain. He didn't need to bargain. If John didn't have the money, another john did, just as there might be another guy willing to go with John to his apartment in Brooklyn, maybe even spend the night. Marco knew he was not going to do that. He felt he went for too little already.

"I think one hundred flat should do it," John said.

"One hundred and overnight?"

John nodded, a smile struggling across his face. Marco smiled back. He had told Jaime that this bar in the East Fifties was good for quick money. He forgot to warn him that the johns haggled like bargain shoppers. If you could wade through the insult of having to negotiate a price, you could usually get the standard. Still, some johns balked and said they never paid more than a hundred, others more than fifty.

Marco took a final swallow of his drink and wiped his mouth. He looked at John and told him, his words flat and spare, that he couldn't do it. Not for a hundred and not overnight.

John let his face hang down toward his glass. It wasn't empty, but he seemed to look at it as if he had drunk too much already. Marco took a step toward the back, but John grabbed his arm and pulled him roughly to his side.

"Oh, all right. One-fifty," he sighed. "I just got paid."

When the cab pulled up to John's apartment building, Marco considered spending the night. The huge stone steps and the polished wood and cut-glass door at the entrance were miles from the dreariness of his own life. His own building had none of the dark wood paneling or rich red carpet winding up the staircase. It was quiet here. No tinny radios playing merengue or quarrels spilling out from behind splintering doors.

Following John into his apartment and catching sight of a cockroach scrambling to one of the unlit rooms, Marco remembered the place wasn't much of an improvement over his own. The paint peeled in the corners and the ceiling had a water stain. The dusty shelves were crammed with cloth-covered books. The scuffed floorboards creaked.

John sat on a piano bench he had pulled out into the middle of the cluttered living room. He stood Marco in front of him, between his legs, and undressed him. Marco looked up at the water stain, trying to figure out what it might look like, but it didn't look like anything. The effort helped him get out of himself though, and his body fell away from him like the clothes now heaped on the floor.

"Look at you," John groaned. "You're beautiful."

His breathing thickened into a series of troubled heaves and he kept grunting the word "beautiful" in a desperate pant as if cast into the predictable drama of a *telenovela*. Marco kept silent and stared at the stain.

John led Marco into the bedroom and laid him down. Marco felt John's hands, rough and calloused, scraping against his body, tearing down his back, to the soles of his feet. Marco did everything he usually did, which was to lie still and pretend he enjoyed it.

For the first time, he thought perhaps he was paid more than what this was worth. A hundred-fifty was a lot for the little he allowed, but then he knew he was more generous than most. Some guys, he heard, only got naked for a hundred-fifty. Everything else was extra. For a hundred-fifty, he gave his johns a round of cheap sex, even kissed those he liked, and those who whined insistently about wanting a kiss. He never loved the johns, but he let himself be loved, which was about the same to most of them in those desperate hours. Still, in this room, looking at the spotty mirror across the dimness, Marco watched himself guiltily. His torso rose up from the tiny bed, legs opened wide, John's head bobbing between his thighs.

When the hour sputtered out, and the room went silent again, Marco got up and dressed to leave. He wanted to head back to the bar. He knew the place would be packed, a doorman stationed at the front, charging a cover, but he wanted to go anyway, to see if Jaime had shown up. John lay in bed, burrowing under the cover of his sheets, and refused to get up. He told Marco to show himself out and shut the door behind him.

The subway train pulled into the Lexington stop, and as Marco waited for the doors to open, he spotted Jaime across the platform. At first he thought he was fooling himself, his body warm with desire, his eyes provoked by a mirage. This couldn't be Jaime, just someone who looked like him. Then Marco got a better look at his face, and the flash of his eyes as they turned to look down the track for the next downtown train. It was Jaime and no one else.

Marco crept up behind him with the thought of pushing aside Jaime's long brilliantined hair and kissing the smooth olive skin of his neck, a compromise for wanting to kiss him on the mouth. The fluorescent lights discouraged everything, though, and he reminded himself that nothing was real yet. He was still limping around with Jaime's name in his shoes.

"So," Marco whispered into Jaime's ear, "you found the bar?"

Jaime spun around, a smirk breaking across his face. "I found it," he said. "You going over there?"

"Nothing else to do."

"I'm hanging it up for tonight."

Despair choked Marco's throat. He needed a glass of water, a sloppy kiss, anything to dissolve the chalky lump. More than anything, he wanted to ask Jaime if he could go home with him, but Jaime became distracted by the approaching thunder of the train.

When the train came to a stop, Jaime got in and Marco remained on the platform. He wanted to follow Jaime, but his legs felt weak, as if the slightest movement would send him stumbling flat onto the concrete. He shoved his hands into his pockets to keep them still. The wad of money John had given him was there.

He traced the edges of a few bills with his fingers. He would have used it all to have Jaime. Of course, he hoped that even if he made the offer, Jaime would decline the money. This was what all johns hoped.

The train conductor called out for the closing doors, and Marco, without words, afraid the proposition might fall out of his mouth and earn him nothing but rejection, put a loose fist to his ear in the shape of a phone. Call, he wanted to say. Jaime understood, but instead of nodding in agreement, he shook his head and pointed back at Marco as the doors shut between them. You call, he mouthed through the window. Marco nodded. The train jerked forward and rumbled down the dark shaft of the tunnel. Marco turned and headed toward the bar, his loneliness like that of the night clerk of the subway token booth, to whom no one paid much attention, or bothered with, who was probably locked in from the outside and had no choice but to sit under the harsh light and wait out the night.

six

The following week, with his knee still troubling him, Marco headed downtown with Jaime under his heels. He still had Jaime's name in his shoes and the stupidity of it flared once more as he buzzed Jaime from the wet street and staggered up the stairs to his apartment. At the door, it struck him that he had forced Jaime to this moment. The invitation to dinner had nothing to do with him or what they had shared that weekend they met at the theater. A wayward saint hovered somewhere and plucked the strings of his cruel harp. Marco hoped to slip into the bathroom, to flush away the paper in his shoes, but after Jaime introduced him to his room-mate, they left the apartment.

They stopped at a liquor store and bought a fat bottle of red wine and headed down to one of the Indian restaurants on Sixth Street. It started to rain but Marco didn't mind. It was Jaime's rush that frustrated him. He walked fast, always a few paces ahead, so that Marco felt dragged along. He had noticed it before, at the theater, but had shrugged it off as Jaime's nervousness. Tonight, Marco lagged behind, feeling pulled like the owner of an apartment-bound dog that had been pent up all day. He hoped the rain would force Jaime to walk by his side, but it only drove him forward, high-stepping under the narrow awnings of the various storefronts along the way.

In the restaurant they squeezed into a rear table. The place looked just like all the others on the block, cheap brass railings out front and rich sitar music inside. The ceiling was a tangled galaxy of twinkling Christmas lights that both cheered the narrow room and threatened to plunge it into darkness with a blown circuit breaker. Marco sat with his back to the door, catching glimpses of the cramped kitchen and the waiters who came in and out with trays of curries and bread. One of the waiters came over and offered to open the wine with a corkscrew but the bottle had a twist-off cap. Jaime took it out of the brown paper bag and poured out two full glasses.

"The wine isn't the best," Jaime admitted, "but it's a lot, and cheap."

"We didn't get the *Nouveau?*" Marco asked.

He thought Jaime would catch the reference to the sign at the hustler bar. He didn't. He gave Marco a half-smile and picked up his glass, rolling the wine around as best as he could. The glass was too full for that. Watching Jaime reminded Marco of all the times he had been out with one of his johns at good restaurants where waiters poured out a few drops of wine for the john to sample before pouring the rest. He never understood why the waiter insisted on performing this pointless ritual. The wine was never bad, so there was never any reason to return it, unless of course the waiter had brought out the wrong bottle, which happened once. This wine tonight would have been sent back if the bouquet, or whatever it was the johns tested, mattered more than the content of the alcohol. To Marco, the wine tasted too much of vinegar, and it made his mouth pucker. He wiped his lips with the napkin to see if it had left a purple stain like cheap punch.

"Not bad," Jaime said. "Want some more?"

"I just took a sip," Marco offered, not knowing if he'd be able to take another, much less finish an entire glass.

"Well, we've got a whole bottle."

"I don't know if I'll be able to finish it."

"Half of it is for me, you know."

Jaime emptied his glass in a simple gulp and poured himself another. A drop of wine dangled from his upper lip. For a moment, Jaime wasn't who Marco had imagined him to be. What had happened to the intense charm? Or had he made that up? A personality he had invented during their time apart? The only clue that Jaime might be who he had been, was his beauty mark, in which Marco cast all his desperate hopes.

"I was waiting for your call," Jaime said. "Or to come by."

"I don't like surprising people when they're not expecting me."

"I really wanted to see you."

"I wanted to see you too. I just figured I'd see you at the theater sometime." Marco hoped to sound as casual as all the other dancers he had known. He tried to mimic their alternating dismissive pitches and alluring tones of voice. "Have you gone back?"

"No. I don't know when I'm going back. I called Olga earlier this week, but she said she didn't know if she could use me." He leaned forward in his seat. "You think she will?"

"Sure. You're a pretty boy."

Jaime's face pulsed with color, though it may have been the lights hanging from the ceiling. He pushed himself back in his seat. "She didn't seem to like me."

"That's just the way she is. I think it's all the pressure she's been getting lately from the city and the police. There are rumors they might shut the place down."

"The cops?"

"The cops are probably the only ones who want to keep it open. There's one guy I know who does all the cops. They all just come to him." Marco suffered through another gulp of his wine. "You never told me about the bar. Was it any good?"

He shrugged. "Not much."

"I don't think I'll be going to the theater for a while. My knee is out. I hurt it last week, running in Central Park." Marco tapped the stem of his wineglass. What to say next? What? "I run to keep myself from waiting by the phone."

"For the johns?"

For you, he thought to himself, and then realized he had said the words aloud as Jaime's face went pink. The blushing color reminded Marco of the paper still in his shoes. He didn't feel so terrible about having cast the spell anymore.

"Running is what I do to keep in shape," he added. "I don't have the patience to go to a gym and work out. It seems monotonous to me."

"You don't get bored running?"

"No way. You've got water, trees, other runners and the Manhattan skyline. I've already picked out two apartment buildings I want to move to on Central Park West."

"After you make your first million?" Jaime smirked. He tipped back in his chair. "I couldn't imagine the number of men I would have to go through to make a million."

"Six thousand," Marco said. "I worked it out." He grabbed his napkin to write out the figures, but he didn't have a pen. He leaned over the table. "You would have to do six thousand men to make a million dollars. Now, it's not so bad if they take you out to a restaurant and a show. I actually like going out like that. I mean, no one else is leaving messages on my machine wanting to take me out. I can't remember the last time I went out like this—on a real date."

The words blared like the sweaty notes of a *mariachi* trumpet. Marco hadn't realized what he'd said until he noticed that Jaime was as still as an empty dance hall, his body slack as a worn streamer, his eyes extinguished. Marco wanted to dig out his own tongue and stomp on it in a clumsy imitation of the Mexican Hat Dance. He hadn't meant to call tonight a real date. He hadn't meant to say it, never mind that it was exactly what he wanted to say, what he wanted to feel most that night, that they were on a romantic date no matter how cheap or casual. He didn't care if the wine had a twist-off cap. He wanted this night to be more than two guys getting together for dinner before getting off.

The waiter placed the sizzling plates of food on the table. The biryani, which Marco had read as rice with almonds and vegetables in a coconut milk sauce, looked like fried rice. He must have ordered the wrong thing. The mound glistened under the lights. The huge samosas looked not much better. They resembled deep-fried butterflies, their breaded wings crumbling into oily flakes.

Marco ate his food hoping the wine would cut most of the grease, as he'd read in newspapers, as one of his johns had told him. Marco drank so much, though, that a sloppy grin smashed against his face. Jaime seemed crippled by the effects of the wine too. He kept blinking, as if to keep his eyes in their sockets. He also let his mouth run reckless, so that when he confessed that he didn't feel handsome enough to be selling himself, he seemed stunned, his face brighter red than any of the twinkling lights in the restaurant. Marco wanted to assure him that he didn't feel pretty either. Working at the theater had taught him that he wasn't pretty enough for some things, or, at least, that not every man found him attractive. He hoped Jaime was not one of them.

"I don't know if I ever want to go back," Jaime said.

"To the theater?"

"Yeah."

"C'mon," Marco insisted, "you're gorgeous."

"It's just kind of scary," he said, his words swollen and warped by the wine. "I've always been afraid of people."

"So how do you meet other men? Or women?"

"It's not like I ever go up to them. They always pick me up."

"You still have to be entertaining. You know, hold up a conversation."

"I've always been afraid," Jaime said. "The theater scares me because it's packed with all these men and I don't know any of them."

"That's what I like about it. That they don't know me. They've pretty much made up their minds about who you are before they even see you. They don't care who you are." Marco took another sip of wine. It tasted better. "They see you, or me, and they've already made up their fantasy—what we like, what we do on our spare time, what we are like in bed. There's this guy who thinks I get off on beating up all of my dates. I only do it to him because he pays me to do it."

"How much?"

"The same."

"Just for hitting him?"

Marco nodded as he broke a corner of the last samosa.

"What do you do to him?"

"Listen to you! You sound like those pervert johns at the bar." Marco imitated the johns in an exaggerated tone: "What can you do? Do you suck? Can I suck you? Can I shove a finger up your ass? Can I shove two fingers up your ass?" He wondered if anyone else, other than Jaime, had heard him. He guessed not. He went on about the john who liked to get beat. "I whip him with a belt or smack him with the back of my hand. Sometimes I'll burn him with matches or melted wax. He thinks I get off on it." Marco leaned across the table. "I never told you this, but he was at the theater the weekend we both worked. He saw us in the duo, and every time I see him now, he's always asking about you. He begs me to tell him what kind of torture you ask for."

"What do you tell him?"

"Whatever he wants to hear. He won't shut up about it. He's always calling and leaving messages about how he dreams about me and the long-haired boy. You're the long-haired boy."

Jaime sat up in his chair, almost proud. "I'm the long-haired boy?"

"Yeah," Marco said, hesitant to say more.

"Maybe he wants to see us together?"

"Forget it."

Jaime laughed. "C'mon, who is this guy?"

"I'm not going to tell you."

"Why not?"

"Because he's a freak," Marco said, to make something up. The truth was Marco didn't want to lose the business to Jaime, as Chris had lost it to Marco the afternoon Chris couldn't make the appointment. It should have been a one-shot deal, but the john hardly called Chris after that. Chris never let Marco forget it.

"Have I seen him before?" Jaime insisted. "Have I?"

"I said forget it. He's got us both wrong." Marco glared at Jaime. "Besides, aren't you supposed to be scared of people?"

He had wanted to make a joke, a mean little one, but Jaime looked hurt, and Marco regretted having said anything. Jaime poured himself another glass of wine. Marco pushed his wineglass away.

"I'm sorry." He sighed. "I should know better. I mean, I'm scared of everything too, including sex. Especially sex."

"That's the only thing that doesn't scare me."

"You didn't have to tell me that," Marco said, almost laughing. "Me, I stayed a virgin until I was nineteen."

"You've probably made up for it by now," Jaime grunted.

"I guess," he said, and pushed his wineglass back toward Jaime, letting him pour him another glass. "I figured I could either work through it or die. You know, work through the fear, like they say in all those self-help books. I mean, you have all these diseases going around and also you wonder whether you're good enough to make someone else feel good or whether someone out there wants you bad enough that they'll pay."

"And you worked through all that?"

"Right." Marco snorted. "I just do it. I don't let it get to me." He sipped his wine and let his eyes linger on the glass. The sides ran as if the glass was crying. "I think I've had a few clients with the virus. I know I have. I've tested months after seeing them, a year, and I'm still negative. That kind of gives me hope that I can still be sexual and enjoy it and not worry about dying."

"How did you know they had it?"

"Just by looking at them, smelling them. You can tell. Besides, I've always felt that the guys with the infections or diseases or the drunks or whomever, the real fucked-up ones, come to us because they have the attitude that if we're fucked up enough to work in this kind of business, and not care about ourselves, why should they?"

"So why do it?"

"Oh, who knows? One john thought I did it because I was afraid of intimacy." Marco laughed. Chris was forever accusing him of that. The reality of it wasn't so much that he was afraid of intimacy, he just hadn't felt capable of it, or hadn't found the right person with whom to share what he felt. Like what he felt now. "The john was buying, right? He was the one who was too afraid, or too lazy, or whatever, to go find someone. And he was saying I was afraid of intimacy?"

"Are you?"

"No," Marco said. He paused. "I do it for the money and for the adventure. Some people jump out of airplanes or climb mountains or swim the Atlantic. Sex has that danger. It comes from the fucking newspapers and television. There's so much bad news that every acronym I spot in a magazine or newspaper spells out AIDS or HIV or KS. I can't look at a single all-cap word without seeing those letters."

"So why do it?" Jaime asked.

"I want to see if I can survive it."

"That's stupid."

"Every reason is," Marco defended. "What's yours?"

"I'm only doing this until I get a real job."

"I think this is as real as it gets."

Jaime smiled. Marco thought Jaime smiled too easily. It didn't seem strained or faked, not even when he spoke through the smile, but it looked odd. Marco wasn't sure he was learning anything about Jaime, or if this night led toward any real future. He wanted to think anything was possible.

When Jaime drank the last of the wine, they paid the check, and stumbled out. Jaime's pace had slowed. His arms dangled at his side. Marco put his arm around Jaime's shoulders and Jaime grabbed Marco by the waist too forcefully for it to have meant anything. He was drunk. Marco felt a little disappointed that it was perhaps not necessarily desire but alcohol that made Jaime touch him. He wanted Jaime to hold him, embrace and smother him with the same passion he felt.

The gates to Tompkins Square Park were still open at that hour, so they cut through it, kicking up the piles of damp leaves fallen from the gnarled and naked trees. All the way to Jaime's place, Marco felt his heart beating, hard as wet cobblestones.

seven

Days later, as Jaime and Marco spent more time together, their relationship unfolding like a map to a beautiful foreign city they were visiting, Jean called and left a message. He was in from Paris and wanted to see Marco. Marco always felt as if Jean had flown in just to see him. Jean made him feel good, and of all the johns he knew, Marco liked him best. He was the only one Marco didn't keep to the clock.

When Marco told Jaime about the appointment, one he would have to go to later that night, Jaime seemed a bit confused, as if just finding out that either of them did this kind of work. It was only work, Marco insisted, and Jaime seemed comforted by the words and the reassuring way in which Marco returned to him on the living room couch. They had been in Jaime's apartment, watching television like fugutives, anxious for news on the outside, but not ready to take part in it. Still, Marco had to take his leave, and as he said his farewell at the door, Jaime suggested that he return afterward for dinner. Marco told him he might not be able to (and he knew for a fact that he could not), because Jean liked to have dinner after his appointments. Marco took a perverse pleasure in the anger that flared Jaime's nostrils. This, he thought, signaled that Jaime cared about him, that their love would only swell to fill the absence.

He took an uptown train to Hell's Kitchen, where Jean lived, and called Jean from a corner pay phone because the apartment buzzer never worked. He hung up after two rings, which Jean had first suggested, to save the quarter.

Jean greeted him with a *bon soir* at the door to the building, and then pointed to his head and grinned. He had once made an obscure joke about hats and now, anytime they met, Jean would point at Marco's head and laugh in a kind of silent running joke. Marco never knew what the joke was but he laughed along anyway and followed Jean up the stairwell.

The apartment was hot and as asphyxiating as a sickroom. A digital thermometer suctioned onto the television screen read eighty degrees. Other thermometers—Jean collected them—hung on the walls. Some were huge, as if they belonged on the sides of red barns in Vermont or rusting gas stations in Arizona. The other walls were decorated with posters of Parisian landmarks and framed pop art of minutely painted caricatures of New York City: a mass of people at Coney Island, a sea of yellow cabs clogging several lanes of traffic, strange outer-galactic creatures climbing the Empire State and Chrysler Buildings. The five radios Jean always had playing throughout the apartment kept the same point on the dial. The songs reminded Marco of growing up with happy dumb music.

Jean brought out a few cans of fruit juice: pineapple and grapefruit and orange. He reminded Marco how to pronounce each in the French. He poured himself a shot of whiskey, which he said had the same name in either language, as if Marco were one of the exchange students he taught at the Sorbonne. Marco obliged him with the lessons. French was a class he'd wanted to take in high school, but was afraid of being called a *maricón*. It was what his father would have called him. Instead, he took Spanish, taught by a gringa teacher from Iowa.

Marco asked Jean if he had any additions to the art and thermometer collection. He thought Jean would just tell him about his rounds at the flea markets. But when he rose to his feet, Marco regretted having asked. It was now going to be a whole show-and-tell.

"Don't get up," Marco called after him.

"But I must," Jean said, already heading to the spare room where he kept his junk not yet on the walls. "I must show you what I found."

He returned with a pair of dinner plates. A smiling bride was painted on one, a serious-faced groom on the other. These weren't the generic faces molded onto the plastic bodies of cake decorations. This couple seemed real, as if they'd had the portraits commissioned to commemorate their historic day.

"You could mix and match," Marco said, wondering if this kind of work was still done, if it was possible to get one made for Jaime and him. He stared into the pale brown eyes of the groom. "You should have gotten two grooms."

"Why?" Jean asked, snatching the plates from Marco's hands.

"I don't know," Marco said, though it seemed obvious to him. Why did Jean want a bride and groom anyway? Two men on dinner plates wasn't any more ridiculous than a straight couple. He didn't say anything, though, just watched Jean take the plates away.

When Jean returned he sat down on the couch with Marco. As always, Jean slumped there without doing anything, though Marco guessed Jean may have felt a bit hurt that he hadn't shared his enthusiasm for the plates. Marco tried to reassure him that the plates were beautiful and asked if he had picked out a particular place on the wall for them. Jean said he had but didn't indicate where.

The clock snapped off the minutes. They continued to sit with nothing happening except the passing of time itself. Marco worried if he'd made the right decision to see Jean. He was thinking he should get through the appointment, forget about dinner, and try to meet up with Jaime later. But Jean was in no rush. He didn't have the infuriating hunger of the other johns, which Marco appreciated, but tonight Marco wished John would do something. He wanted to come and get out of there, so he did what he never did, he initiated the sex act. He touched Jean's hand, stroking the gray hairs on his pale liver-spotted arms to prime his libido, and then went on to unbutton his shirt and unbuckle his belt and pull off his pants. A few snappy songs later, they lay in the bedroom, Jean's arm around him, his scratchy chest against Marco's side. Jean's chest always disturbed him with its suspicious dark moles and flat moons, but Marco had learned to work with it, going so far as to take Jean's nipples in his teeth, anything to make him come faster because Jean invariably wanted to make it last. All the johns did.

The radios echoed through the apartment. The DJ was taking requests and dedications, and one of the first she announced, a song something of an anthem of love, forced Marco back to junior high. He couldn't remember the name of the song or the singer but the familiar music swelled with a deep passion and Marco thought of Jaime and all the years he'd spent without him. How strange that he hadn't existed for him then.

At the start of the next song Marco got up to shower. Jean usually insisted Marco remain in bed for a while, but tonight, perhaps numbed from the orgasm he seemed to have suffered like a minor heart attack, he wiped himself with a washcloth and then lay back down. Marco used one of the other washcloths to shower. Jean had a collection of them too. They were all new and used only once to clean up after sex. Jean discarded them in the trash cans out on the street. His habit, whether it was a precaution against disease, or to save himself the embarrassment of taking the stained cloths to the Chinese laundry, made Marco laugh and wince at the extraordinary waste.

Marco returned to his clothes on the living room couch. He tried to figure a way to get out of dinner. He could say he wasn't feeling well, that he was tired, but he thought any excuse would come out forced and false. From the living room, he glanced at Jean still in bed, his flat ass turned toward him like a dim smile. He regretted having upset him about the plates.

"You should get one of those plates done for you," Marco said, putting on his clothes.

Jean rolled over and faced him. "Perhaps when I get married."

Marco thought Jean was only playing along with the joke, though he couldn't tell, never could, from the blank expression on his face. Jean called it his "English humor." Marco pressed on, venturing that he hoped to get an invitation, maybe a spot of honor, in the wedding party.

"Oh, quite definitely," Jean said, propping himself up on an elbow. "But the wedding won't be for a few years."

"Are you marrying French or American?"

"French, of course! My mother would have an attack if I had American."

Jean made it sound like a choice of food. He could either have the escargot in a garlic-butter sauce or a burger and fries. Marco guessed Jean's mother would flat-out die if Jean married a man. Yet he couldn't imagine him with anyone else. He was so used to hearing Jean compliment him on his "nice piece," asking him if he could "suck it a little," that trying to imagine what he might say to a woman was as far from his head as the romantic city of Paris. Maybe Jean dated only women in Paris. Marco didn't know.

"In my background," Jean began, and then paused. "In the dream—it's like a dream, really—I always see a French woman. This woman I know. A friend of the family."

"So why haven't you married her yet?" Marco asked.

Jean shrugged. "She's old and boring. She hates going to the mountains to ski. She absolutely abhors the United States. I don't think she would let me come here to New York once I married her."

"She sounds wonderful," Marco said, buckling his belt, not meaning a word of what he was saying.

"Maybe she's not so nice," Jean said. "Maybe she's not perfect, but I think people who don't have a family are terribly alone. I think about it. It would be nice sometime to have a wife and children. Marriage is a security. It gives you a kind of social security with other people and your work and friends. Two men can't make a family. Not really. They might love each other, maybe, but if they die, that's it. Nobody cares."

Marco fell onto the couch. He faced one of the thermometers, a give-away from a Midwestern bank, keeping silent record of the temperature. He didn't want to say anything, afraid he might heatedly point out to Jean that he was too old to get married, to have children, to finally give in to societal pressures. He was what? Fifty-five? Sixty? Why give up now, Marco wanted to ask. Why settle for the cinderblock prison of security over the sand castles of love, he thought, sounding like one of the syrupy songs from the radio.

"You don't think two men can love each other?" Marco defended. In the last week, after their dinner date, he and Jaime had shared a chain of days in which nothing mattered more than being in each other's arms. If it wasn't for Jean's call, they would still have been together that night. He doubted Jean had ever experienced anything like that. At a hundred-fifty an hour, it would have cost him a fortune.

Jean said, "Two men in love is a selfish kind of love. And then I think it gets boring. The love needs to turn into something else or it just dies. A man and a woman, they can have a child and they can give the love they had for each other to that child."

"And if two men adopted?" Marco had never considered adopting. He only mentioned it to keep the debate going.

Jean got up from the bed. He scratched his armpits and yawned. Marco thought he had beaten Jean on this point, but then Jean spoke and said that adopting wasn't so good.

"If they take a boy," he said. "There's the risk that the boy grows up, gets to ten or fifteen or twenty and they fall in love with the boy. It's better they get a girl, but even then it might not be so good for her growing up. There are suddenly many risks. Dangers. Because the child is not from you, if I can say. They're not of your blood."

Jean yawned again, checking his watch, confirming the radio announcement that it was the bottom of the hour, and he moved toward the bathroom, saying he'd made dinner reservations at their usual spot. Marco wanted to shoot back some flaming arrow of fact to defend his point about men in love. It was possible, he wanted to shout. It could last.

He felt defenseless, without weapon, without one burning experience on which to draw. The sweat poured out of him from the heat in the room, but he was ready to jump into the senseless fight of a spurred rooster. The argument had brought him back to the nights his father would stumble home from the *cantinas*. Los Chamacos had broken up, and his father had been forced back to his old job of wiring homes. He'd wake Marco, even if it was past midnight, and force him into a kitchen chair to watch him eat dinner. Marco would sit, feeling his gut thicken and go cold. He'd grow old, his father lectured, as he picked his plate, and would suffer as he had, from whatever *sueños* he kept, whatever dreams he aspired to. His father told him he would do him the favor of breaking him like a mule, ridding him of his dreams before they broke him. For this Marco would thank him later. Now Jean was doing the same thing to him, beating down his passion to an impotent stump.

In high school, Marco remembered, everyone decorated their books with their fierce pronouncements of who they loved and punctuated them with the challenge *¡Y Que!* He thought of ways to translate it so that Jean might understand, but in English it didn't sound as defiant, and in French he had no clue.

Out on the cold street, making their way to the restaurant, Jean *sautéed le coque á l'ane,* what he called talking about everything from the chicken to the donkey. He reported that another bomb had been detonated in the Paris Métro. He blamed the Algerians. He said his mother wanted him to drive her and the maid to Portugal so that the maid could visit her family. Beautiful country, he added, but completely undeveloped, and poor, so that he could get things cheap. Marco wondered how much the boys went for in Lisbon and where they would stand in Jean's exhaustive collection of boys. Where did he?

On the sidewalk, as they waited for the cross light, he noticed an underdressed guy. The guy seemed more interested in showing off his body than keeping it warm. Marco locked eyes with him, and he nodded. It didn't matter that they had never met. They both recognized what they were. Marco watched him pass, thinking he might turn around, though he didn't know for what. When the guy disappeared into the crowd, Marco turned back to Jean,

103

but Jean was already in the middle of the crosswalk. As he sprinted up to him, Marco noticed, for the first time since leaving the apartment, that Jean was carrying the paper bag with the sticky washcloths.

"I lived with someone once," Marco said, his breath burdened from the run. He was getting out of shape. "We were together two years."

"But you were both young."

"I was nineteen."

"And he was older? Or the same age?"

"Older," Marco said, hoping Jean wouldn't ask whom it was. Jean never liked Chris. He always said Chris was a bit "fatty," and added that when Chris danced, as if staking the perimeter of the stage with his strut, he scowled as if the men in the audience were sacks of garbage. When Jean first mentioned it, Marco was shocked that the near belligerence and condescension with which Chris treated everyone, and him especially, was so obvious. Why was it not as apparent to him when they first met? Was he that young? He remembered, "I was nineteen and he was twenty-four."

"Twenty-four," Jean repeated with a laugh. "It's the same, nineteen and twenty-four. Maybe because you were so young you thought five years is a lot of time, but when you're forty, or my age, you'll see that nineteen and twenty-four is the same." He stopped at the corner and dropped the crumpled bag into a trash can. "When you are a child—a young person, suddenly—you have some things in common with the other person you love. You are alike. You want to be with them. But, it doesn't last. It can't last for more than three or four years at most because those things you have that are the same are not so interesting anymore and you can't make them interesting."

Marco argued that he knew a couple that had been together for thirty years. He was talking about Quentin, the john who liked to get beat and was continually troubled by the relationship with his partner. Of course, he wasn't going to tell Jean all that. Marco just wanted to make his point.

"Thirty years," Jean repeated. They had arrived at the restaurant and Jean was looking at the daily specials posted on the glass doors. "Yes, well, thirty years, those are people from a different time. They had a fight, if I can say. Fighting against the society tastes." He turned to Marco. "That makes a kind of link your age can't have. It's too free now. You aren't fighting for anything, so it's easier to just get bored and fight each other."

Jean held the door open for Marco but Marco hesitated. Was it Chris who had once derided the restaurant as a place where secretaries, with their secretary friends, celebrated their promotions, or commiserated about their affairs and impending divorces? It could have been no one else, since he was always bragging about the amount of money, the bloated number of hours, he and Richard could spend at various restaurants. These other places, places that did not get reviewed, he remembered Chris saying, were everyday events. For Marco they meant more, but tonight he felt his enthusiasm drained.

He tried to invent an excuse for not entering the restaurant, but what could he say, and besides he had nowhere else to go. Jaime would have already gone out to dinner. Marco figured he might as well go eat. He stepped into the restaurant and held the second door for Jean to enter first. As much as he liked the place, Marco was unsettled by the faces that would turn to eye him, and then Jean, returning to whatever they were eating once their story had become as plain as the white butcher paper on the tables. He rarely went out in public with the johns because of this. Everyone knew what they were, what they had just done, or were about to. Marco only let his resistance lag with Jean because he counted him as a friend and knew they could sustain a conversation. They knew one another well enough to make the other diners doubt their initial assumptions.

The host sat them by the windows facing the street. From the table, they also had an unobstructed view of the restaurant. Its walls were hung with large prints of fedoras painted in bright primary colors: a yellow hat against a blue background, a red against green, a white against black. Jean came here a lot. He didn't cook at home, but he loved food and he'd told Marco that he liked taking him to dinner because he appreciated how much Marco enjoyed eating. He didn't eat as fast and as quietly as the other

Americans he knew. Marco assumed the other Americans were other hustlers, though Jean never spoke of seeing anyone else.

"I hope we don't get the waiter who's missing the brain," Jean said, looking over the menu. "The last time I was here, the waiter with the thick glasses suddenly took away the appetizer and asked if I wanted dessert or coffee. He was positively mad."

Marco had been with Jean that night the waiter forgot the entrees. He didn't remind him of it though. He was worrying about Jaime again, thinking he had made the wrong decision in choosing to spend the evening with Jean. He didn't want Jaime to change his mind about him. Not now. Not as he was realizing that Jaime was whom he hoped for. These nights with the johns had been nothing but practice.

"Don't look so melancholic," Jean said, flashing a rare smile and pressing the butcher paper flat against the table, as if it might smooth out the rest of the night. "I didn't mean to make life sound so black. Next time we see each other, you tell me all the contrary. Tell me about that couple you know that's been together thirty years. They sound fascinating."

After dinner, Jean walked Marco to the subway. Marco shook Jean's hand goodnight and then took the steps down to the trains. The grinding noise of the approaching trains, their steel wheels against the track, wore him down to a raw and aching fatigue. He felt like going home to sleep, but decided to head downtown to Jaime's place. Nothing Jean had said, and nothing Marco had experienced before, mattered as much as being with Jaime tonight.

Marco thought he knew about love, thought he was in the business of it, but of course he wasn't. The business laughed at it and dared it to exist, just as every relationship seemed to as well. The years he had spent with Chris, the broken lives of the johns, it was all a sad joke on love. Watching the bare light bulbs shoot past, and the pale reflections of sparks flashing under the rocking train, Marco realized that he had no clue what love was. He had never seen it, had never felt it, had never tasted it in his mouth. With Jaime he only hoped love was possible.

eight

Love was like the L-train. Both took a long time coming and sometimes Marco just wanted to give up on it. He had never felt this desperation before because love had never mattered. It had never been a part of his vocabulary, just as the L-train had never been a train he took, until he met Jaime who lived so far east that the avenues dropped their numbers for letters of the alphabet. The only way to get to Jaime's place was on the L.

Marco would have invited Jaime to his own place, but when he first moved in with Soledad, he had agreed not to bring strangers home. The last person who lived with her had brought home everyone he met at the bars. Their phone and beeper numbers were inked into the wall by the bed, on the bed frame itself, and on numerous scraps of paper Marco had pulled out from behind the vanity when he first moved in. Sol said she never cared what the guy did with his life—though she added that he was now dead from AIDS—until a trick he brought home one night robbed them.

He tied them up in the living room and took off with the television and stereo and toaster oven. She warned Marco that she didn't want to get robbed again, she'd just bought new appliances, so he agreed not to bring guests to the apartment.

Marco didn't have a problem with it. He had just made the break from Chris and didn't feel like getting involved with anyone. He didn't want to get serious until he was ready to leave the business. At some point, Sol's rules relaxed, probably when she began smoking in all the rooms. Marco fell back with Chris and Chris began coming to the apartment. Chris and Sol got along. They both loved to smoke and dish like bitchy queens.

Now Marco was worried about Jaime. He wanted to bring Jaime home because he was growing tired of going to his place in the East Village. The whole trip, including transfers, took over an hour each way. The L felt as if transit workers were only now laying the track for the train to roll forward. Marco wanted to know if Jaime would suffer the same grueling ride to see him. He hoped Sol wouldn't prove too big an obstacle, but even if she didn't mind, he couldn't just have Jaime spend the night. He had to buy new sheets first. Washing the ones he slept with weren't going to help them look any better. The paisley-print flat was old, borrowed from Chris when Marco first moved out of the hotel, and the other sheet, black faded to gray, belonged to Sol.

Marco woke up early one morning and went to a downtown department store. He got there before the store even opened and waited to buy a set of floral print sheets and two feather pillows. He bulleted home, shoved the sheets into the washer the landlord wasn't supposed to know about, and called Jaime at once. He left a message for him to come uptown that afternoon. When he hung up, the phone rang. He figured it was Jaime calling back, but it turned out to be Chris. Marco had not spoken with him in the last several weeks and almost didn't recognize his voice.

Out on the roof of the apartment building, the shouts and screams from the schoolkids playing in the nearby basketball court shot through the air like pebbles cast from slings. The kids were having recess and seemed louder than the midday traffic on the street below. Chris was saying nothing at all, as if he'd spent all he had to say on his phone call. He stood holding the damp sheets in his arms as Marco pinned them to the line strung up between the pipe vents.

"You think it'll dry?" Marco asked.

"The sun's out," Chris said, offering the obvious.

"Incredible weather for winter."

"I'm sure the fags love it. A few days to wear hot pants."

"I thought you'd be wearing yours."

"Don't get ugly."

Marco hung the pillowcases and sat down in the red vinyl chair he'd brought up to the roof last summer, when he had nothing better to do than watch the sun set over the river and slide past Jersey. The chair smelled moldy from the rains. Chris sat on a piece of cardboard, his face to the sun, as if he were at the Christopher Street piers getting a tan. He loved to tan, no matter how carcino- genic it was.

"I don't know where to begin," Chris said.

"About?" Marco asked, the sun stroking his arms. "Is it Nathan?"

"I don't know how to get into this without it sounding too mat- ter of fact. I mean, anything I tell you has happened over the last, what, six weeks?" Chris looked up at Marco. "It was draining— emotionally and physically." Chris forced a weak smile, as if more would hurt his face. "Did I tell you I got sick and had to stay in bed a few days?"

"I don't know anything," Marco said, feeling his body strained from sitting in the chair and the effort he made to listen for the phone in the apartment. He didn't want to miss Jaime. "You haven't called."

"You couldn't call me?"

"You said you didn't want me to call you."

"You could check on me every once in a while. See if I'm still alive."

"You're like a cockroach. You'll outlive everyone."

"Don't apologize," Chris said, crossing his arms, a grim smile full on his lips. "So, let's see. Chris and his current situation in five minutes or less." He squinted at the tar roof and then back at

Marco. "Nathan, that on-and-off lover of mine, still has his lover. I don't know why he has to be so damned responsible and sensitive. Why can't he just leave him? They're in couples therapy. He and I should be in couples therapy. Anyway, I told you I got sick, right?"

"You didn't say what it was."

"I didn't know what it was. It felt like a fever or something. My stomach hurt. I hurt all over and then I got this swelling down there."

"Front or back?"

"Back. I just thought they were hemorrhoids. So I went to the drugstore and bought some Preparation-H. A few days passed and it only got worse. I couldn't take a shit after a while because it hurt so bad. I went to the clinic and they swabbed me up and sent the specimen to the lab. They couldn't do anything until they got the results. I get them next week, I think. Anyway, it got to the point where I couldn't even sit down and I was really afraid to go to the bathroom so I went to another clinic, but they were closed for some stupid city holiday. By that time, I had to tell Nathan and he called up his short list of doctors and made an appointment for me to see one during my lunch hour. I went in and the doctor told me I had an outbreak of herpes."

"Herpes?"

"I've had them before," he said.

"Herpes?" Marco shot back. "When?"

"A while ago. I don't know, maybe last summer." Chris pushed himself up from the cardboard and paced the roof. "The doctor took care of it and I went back to work and then Adam was waiting for me in the lobby and I went to lunch with him because I needed to talk to someone."

"Do I know Adam?"

"He's not important," Chris said. "We slept together a few times. That's all."

"Did you tell him?"

"Are you kidding?"

"Don't you think he should know?" Marco's voice rose.

"I'll tell him later." Chris raised his voice to match Marco. "If he

110

gets it, I'll tell him, but I don't think he will. We hardly did anything. Maybe he gave it to me."

"Even more reason to tell him."

"This isn't about Adam," Chris shouted. The playground noise subsided, as if all the kids had stood to watch a boy sobbing in the corner of the schoolyard. Chris sighed. He turned his face to the sky, and then back to Marco. "The point is that after the doctor, I went out to lunch with Adam and forgot to call Nathan back. When I got back to the office, I couldn't call him from my desk because I didn't want everybody to hear about it, and then during a run for coffee, I couldn't find a pay phone that didn't have the receiver ripped out of it. Nathan called me at home later and I must have been tired from the drugs because he asked me why I didn't call him after the appointment with the doctor, and I said that I had gone out to lunch with Adam. I'd said a few peripheral things about Adam before, mostly to make him jealous, but this time Nathan just flipped out. He hung up on me. I called back, but he said he didn't want to get into it, that obviously I had things I had to work out for myself." Chris paused. "It was like this guy who used to think the world of me suddenly—"

"Suddenly what?"

"Suddenly didn't care. Just like that, he turned off like a light bulb. He said he could be there for me as a friend but nothing else. I told him that to become friends, so many things had to get broken, so many emotions killed off, that we could never go back to being lovers. I hung up crying. He called me back crying and told me that he didn't want to lose what we had together. I promised never to see Adam again, to get counseling, clean up."

"And the herpes?"

"The herpes thing is easy. It's not terminal. I mean, Nathan's lover is positive, so herpes is like having acne." Chris rubbed a freckle on his arm. "Anyway, the first outbreak is usually the worst and it slowly becomes less severe and less frequent."

"But it lasts forever." Marco leaned forward. "You can't get rid of it."

"Listen, you don't die from it."

No, Marco thought, you don't die from it, but he had always

111

been afraid when they were together that Chris would get something you could die from and pass it to him. Chris almost seemed to want it, as if he thought himself immune, or hoped, maybe, that impending death would keep them together, closer than love ever could. Marco looked back at Chris and shook his head. "When did you first notice the symptoms?"

"A couple weeks ago," Chris said.

"No," Marco clarified, "the first time."

"Last summer, I guess, around graduation."

"You've had sex with me since then."

"Don't worry. It's not that contagious."

"It's not that contagious?" Marco repeated, getting up, ready to scratch the words onto the side of the building like a dazzling work of graffiti. "It's not *that* contagious he says!"

"Not unless it's active," Chris pleaded. "That's what the doctor said. He said I couldn't give it to another person unless it was active. And I can usually feel it coming. I get this itchy feeling and that means it's coming." Chris seemed spent, drained by his need to be understood. "I would never do anything to hurt you."

"You said that about the warts," Marco said.

"I didn't know I still had them. I never meant to give them to you."

Marco edged over to the side of the building and looked over at the school yard. The blacktop was empty. The kids had gone back inside. Gone were the playful shouts and sing-song taunts, the soft thud of basketballs and rope skipped, of teachers whispering among themselves.

"Are you going to be okay?" Marco asked. His words felt as false and useless as fake money. "Is there something I can do?"

"No," Chris said, stepping toward Marco, then retreating to the damp sheets hanging on the clothesline. "I just have to be more careful. And it's not like I went out looking for it either. I know it sounds like an excuse, but I should explain, you know, so that you won't think I'm, like, trying to kill myself. It just happened. It was the other guy who insisted and pushed it. And it's not like he came inside me or anything." Chris paused, as if to think about it a moment, as if listening to his words echo between the buildings.

"I know, I know, I know. He doesn't have to come in order for it to be dangerous, but it just happened. It's insane and inexcusable."

"So why do it?" Marco challenged.

"Because it's there? I'm tired of having to say no all the time. I always deny myself. For once, I just want to feel what it's like again." The sun slid behind a cloud, a luminous island of white in the blue sea of sky. "I'm reading this book. The guy wrote it as he was dying. It reads very matter-of-fact, almost glib, but again and again he writes about how much he had enjoyed his life and that death didn't seem so unfair."

"How old was he?"

"Fifty, maybe."

"Fifty." The fat number rolled off Marco's lips. "You just hit thirty. There's no comparison. You have a shit job at a television company and live in a hole. You call that a life?"

"It's not a shit job and I like the hotel," Chris said, as if he needed to convince himself of it. He turned away and then laughed into the air. "I like my life," he said, more sure of himself. "It's not like I'm forced to yank on any more diseased dicks for a few dollars."

"Guess not," Marco said, and he wondered in one unexpected moment of inspiration where he had put that résumé they had written together. Maybe a shit job wasn't so bad.

nine

The snow came down like clumps of refrigerated rice. It didn't stick to the sidewalks, but melted as soon as it hit, as if the concrete was cold enough to burn away everything. Marco pushed his way east on Thirteenth Street to where Jaime lived. Nothing cheered him as he walked, not the holiday lights wrapped around the fire escapes of the surrounding buildings, not the tinny sounds of radios drifting from behind the frost-covered windows. The tropic beats of salsa and merengue were stunted by the chill he felt taking residence at the bottom of his spine, a cold sweat dampening the crack of his ass. When he got to Jaime's building, he pressed the buzzer hard, wanting to burst right through the heavy gray doors.

Jaime lived on the second floor, in a front apartment that faced the squats across the street. A congress of poor artists and bohemians had scrapped together living quarters in the abandoned tenement, which city officials decried as illegal, but the squatters didn't seem to bother anyone. The only irritating thing was that they probably lived no worse than anyone else on the street and paid not a dollar of the inflated rents. Where Jaime lived, there was no elevator, or much heat, so Marco took the stairs fast and hurried down the hall, pulling off his gloves and breathing into his hands. Jaime's door hung open and Jaime pushed his face through, first smiling, then something less.

"Are you all right?" he asked Marco.

Marco nodded and went in. He stood against the sink in the kitchen and let Jaime kiss him. Despite Jaime's warm lips and the embrace, Marco still felt a chill crawl over his body, like cold-limbed insects trapped under his clothes. When he pulled away Marco could see that Jaime had sensed his lousy mood.

"There's soup on the stove," Jaime said, with as much enthusiasm as a waitress at the end of her shift. "It's cold. You should have come sooner."

"I had things to do," Marco said, as Jaime moved away to the bedroom. Looking into the pot, Marco guessed there was enough food to start a soup line or feed the men who lived in both Tompkins Square Park and under the bridge of Riverside Drive near his apartment. Thinking about the men made Marco less hungry. He just wanted to lie down. He hoped Jaime wouldn't ask him questions. He didn't want to lie. He didn't want to tell him about the last three hours, spent in a Park Avenue hotel room with Quentin. Would Jaime even remember Quentin? Quentin had remembered him. The long-haired boy, he called him. He wouldn't shut up about how he wanted to meet him. Marco kept saying one day he might just bring him as a surprise. Of course, he never would. That was the thing about the business. You had to keep them wanting. Otherwise they never called you again.

Jaime came back to the living room wearing a pressed shirt open a few buttons. He asked Marco if he'd had some of the soup yet, eyeing him with suspicious glances, and then not at all.

"It looks great," Marco said, joining him by the couch. "But I'd rather have a hot bowl of you. I've been thinking of you all day."

Marco kissed him, but Jaime didn't seem to kiss back.

"Are you going to wear that to the party?" he asked.

Marco remembered the party. A clothes store on Fifth Avenue was previewing its spring line. Jaime had mentioned wanting to go for the free drinks. Marco had on his college flunkie uniform of ripped jeans and a black nylon jacket with a bright orange lining, which Quentin liked, but Jaime didn't. Jaime wore good clothes, the kind you only sent to the cleaners.

"I got some extra clothes if you need it," he said and got up. "C'mon, get ready."

"You sure you wanna go out?" Marco asked, still on the couch. "In this weather?"

"Yes," Jaime said. "It'll only be for a little while. It's not like we're going to stay out all night."

"I don't feel too good," Marco said, which was half true.

"Not even for an hour?"

"Can't you go without me?"

An annoyed twitch hooked a corner of Jaime's lip and he looked down at his fingers and scraped under his nails.

"Are you really sick?" he asked.

"I'm getting there," Marco said, pretending to stagger up off the couch. He stumbled and banged his shin against the coffee table. He felt he deserved it and fell back on the couch.

Jaime sat with him, massaging his leg. "Do you have a fever?"

"I don't know," Marco said, putting a hand to his forehead, and then turning toward Jaime with an exhausted laugh.

"Fine." Jaime dropped Marco's leg. "Are you going home?"

"You want me to?"

"No." He let out a tired rush of air. "I want you to stay."

"You do?"

"Yeah, you idiot. Stay here until I get back. One drink and I'll be home. All right?"

"And your roommate?"

"He's gone to his girlfriend's in Brooklyn. He's not coming back."

"You sure?" Marco asked, and watched Jaime prepare to go out. Marco didn't know whether he wanted to stay or not. Maybe he was getting sick, maybe he was still shaking off the violence of that afternoon with Quentin which never was his scene, but the thought of Jaime coming home later, to have sex, or whatever, left him nauseated. Anytime he spent the night, sex was a part of it, but lately he'd wanted less of it and more of something else, though he didn't know what. Maybe what he wanted was the security that Jaime still desired him even if they didn't have sex.

Marco woke up sour-mouthed and alone. Jaime had left him on the couch with the suggestion that he put on a pair of pajamas and get into bed, but he was in the living room, wearing his still damp clothes. He stretched out on the couch, in the hard light of the living room lamp, and scratched his head, letting his hand fall limp across the back of his neck and over the slope of his shoulders. He felt better now that he had slept. Perhaps it had only been a momentary nap that he needed. How many minutes? He checked the clock on the stereo. A quarter past midnight. Jaime should have been back by now. Marco stumbled into the bedroom to see if he had returned, but other than the ordered mess on the floor, the pajama pants folded on the bed, the room was empty. Through the window, the sodium halos of the streetlights were glowing.

A rattling of keys came from the door. Marco recognized Jaime's mutterings and crossed the apartment to let him in, but the door opened before he reached it, and Jaime fell in, almost stumbling to the floor. His hand seemed stuck to the doorknob.

"My keys," he slurred.

Marco went over and pulled the keys out and shut the door. Jaime came up and kissed him, his coat damp and cold, his hair stiff and icy.

"I missed you," Jaime said, leaning into Marco. "Did you miss me?"

"Yes," he said. Jaime's slurred words were unsettling.

"I had no one to talk to."

"Your friends didn't go?"

"I had no one good to talk to," he said, striking his fists softly against Marco's chest, pulling on the neck of Marco's shirt so that he could kiss him again. "Did you miss me?"

"I said yes." Marco drew his head to the side, not wanting to kiss Jaime full on the mouth. He smelled of cigarettes and liquor.

Jaime seemed hurt by the sudden movement and he pulled back, the drops of melted snow dripping from his hair into his red-rimmed eyes. He looked down at his feet where the water was puddling.

"You're not lying to me?" he asked, turning to Marco.

"Lying? About what?"

"About missing me."

"No," Marco said, almost laughing because it struck him as funny, the pleading drunken voice Jaime used, its shaken confidence. Marco grabbed Jaime's hands, to pull him in close, but Jaime stepped to the stove and looked into the cold pot of soup. He took a spoonful, a pale noodle sticking to the bottom of his lip, which he didn't seem to notice.

"My friends wanted to meet you," he said. "They wanted to know who I was hanging out with."

"Hanging out?" Marco repeated. He got behind Jaime and let Jaime feed him some soup. "Is that what we're doing? Hanging out with each other?"

"Yeah," he said with a mouthful.

"And what does hanging out actually mean?"

"What we're doing right now."

"Eating cold soup?"

"Eating cold soup and spending the night together."

"Is that what you told your friends?"

"Did I leave something out?" he asked and fed Marco another spoonful.

Marco slurped it down and said nothing. He wished Jaime had told his friends that he had a boyfriend, and that he planned to move in with him soon, to live happily ever after. Then again, at least he'd told them they were spending the night. That counted for something. Since moving to New York, he couldn't count the number of men who had pushed him out of their apartment once they'd gotten off—not the johns, who wanted him to stay, but the guys he wanted to be with, other dancers and regular guys he met at the bars. They gave him excuses about having to work the next day, or to meet a lover, or had simply gotten what they wanted and didn't need him further but thank you.

"Hey," Jaime said, tapping the cold spoon against Marco's fore-head. "Wake up."

"Did you have a good time at the party?" Marco asked. "How was it?"

"The usual crowd." Jaime shoved the pot into the fridge. The soup seemed to have sobered him up. "There's never anyone new in New York. It's always the same people at the same parties with the same stories."

"So why go?"

"Because," he said on the way to the bedroom, "you never know."

The remark should have upset Marco, but because Jaime laughed it off, he laughed too. He followed Jaime into the bed-room and stood at the door, watching him struggle with his shoes in the dark. He was trying to remove them without untying the laces. Marco stepped in to help as Jaime lay spent on the bed.

"When am I going to meet your friends?" Jaime asked.

"My friends?" Marco asked.

"Yeah. Do you even have friends?"

"No." The laces seemed to be in knots. "Not really."

"You don't have any friends?" Jaime repeated and sat up.

Marco thought for a moment. "Okay," he admitted, lifting Jaime's foot out of the shadows so that he could untie the laces. "I have one. One friend."

"One? I don't believe you."

"I'm always working," Marco explained. He removed one shoe and then the other. "And when I'm not working, everyone else is. I'm on another schedule. Besides, what am I going to tell my friends when they ask me about what I did today? Uhm, well, let's see, I got sucked off by two fat guys this morning, had lunch, and beat one up late in the afternoon."

"My friends all want to know how I've been managing between jobs. They think I'm getting help from my dad." He shrugged and began removing his coat. "Am I going to meet your one friend?"

"Not if I can help it."

"Has he got something on you I shouldn't know about?"

"He's an ex-boyfriend."

"You're still friends with him?"

"Yeah." Marco helped Jaime out of his coat and then his shirt. The feel of Jaime's smooth body was so different from the crepe-skinned men from the theater. Even Chris's skin wasn't as soft to the touch. Marco knew he would never introduce the two of them to each other because Chris would want Jaime for himself. Jaime had those dark looks that would draw his interest.

Jaime went on about his friends, his words fading, body going slack. As he slept, his body seemed enshrined in the glow from the street lamps.

Marco got up to hang Jaime's coat, but when he turned around, Jaime was behind him, reaching for the coat and searching its pockets.

"I left the keys on the counter," Marco offered, but it wasn't what Jaime said he wanted.

"There was a box in one of the pockets," Jaime whimpered, still fumbling through his coat as Marco changed into pajamas. When Jaime seemed to find what he needed, he dropped the coat on the floor and came behind Marco with a thin silver box in his hands. It glimmered in the dimness.

"That for me?" Marco asked, since Jaime had said nothing.

"Yeah," he said. "I got it this afternoon."

Marco reached for it, but Jaime snatched it back.

"Did you buy it for me or for you?"

"For you." Jaime handed the box to him. "You have to keep it here, though. You can't take it with you."

Marco looked at the narrow box, at the silver angels etched on the wrapping paper, with trumpets against their mouths. He couldn't imagine that there would be anything more inside than a couple of sharpened pencils. He glanced at Jaime, unsure if he should open it right then, or wait until Christmas a few days away.

"Open it," Jaime said, sitting back on the bed, watching.

Marco peeled the paper until he was left with a clear plastic case, and in it, a green-handled toothbrush with red bristles. He kept turning the case in his hands, thinking back on all the flowers and candies and dinners the johns had given him. Some gifts he loved, some he merely appreciated, but the toothbrush, an

121

instrument of the ordinary, the everyday, meant more than he could have ever hoped. The toothbrush meant Jaime wanted him. In his apartment and life to the hereafter.

"It's nothing," Jaime said.

"It's not nothing. It's a toothbrush." Marco crawled onto the bed and kissed Jaime on the mouth. "I'll go use it right now."

Jaime laughed. "Is that the thanks I get?"

"I didn't mean anything bad about your mouth. You taste wonderful," he lied. He kissed him again, twice, and then went into the bathroom.

The times Marco had spent the night at Jaime's, he only rinsed his mouth with mouthwash, or if his mouth was especially rank, as it usually was in the morning, teeth dingy from coffee, he'd use his finger to brush his teeth. He always forgot to bring his own brush and never thought to buy himself one and leave it at the apartment. As he brushed tonight, watching himself in the mirror, Marco kept smiling to himself. He knew where he stood now with Jaime. They belonged together, like their toothbrushes propped up side by side in a mason jar. It was more than official. They were practically living together.

When Marco returned to bed, Jaime was snoring. Marco looked at him, trying not to feel guilty for once thinking Jaime was nothing but a capricious straight boy who wanted to see what it was like to be with another guy. He figured the story about the girlfriend had been a lie because as far as he had seen, on the numerous nights they had spent at Jaime's apartment, there was never any evidence of there having been anyone else before him. There were no photos or ribbon-tied letters or even phone calls from women. He turned out the lamp in the living room and crawled into bed. Jaime moved toward him, wrapping his arms around him, sharing his warmth.

Marco kissed him on the temple and whispered into his ear. "I've been saving money," he said, not knowing if he was awake enough to hear him. "I want to get out of here. Go somewhere. Mexico maybe. Or the Philippines. Do you know the Philippines?"

As if reading from an encyclopedia, Jaime mumbled, "The Philippines. There are over seven thousand islands, half unnamed, and only nine hundred habitated. That's all I know."

"You have family there?"

"My father goes there now and again to visit his brothers."

"Is it beautiful?"

"I've never been there." He moved in closer, resting his head on Marco's chest. "Never been there."

"It's kind of like me," Marco said, stroking Jaime's hair. "I've never really been to Mexico. One or two border towns now and then with my folks, but supposedly that's not Mexico." He remembered how Chris used to say he wasn't really Mexican. He wasn't dark enough, and he made love like an amateur. He lifted Jaime's face to his. "Hey," Marco said, his voice urgent, "let's get away—the both of us."

"Sure," Jaime said, his eyes still shut. "I could be into something like that."

Marco let Jaime's head rest. "I've got two thousand saved up."

"Two thousand?" Jaime asked, as if distracted by the more vivid panorama of his dreams. "Two thousand could get us a house and servants in Manila. If we saved a bit more, we could stay there a while. A few more weekends for us—you at the theater, me at the bar, and we'll be set."

"I'm not going back to the theater," Marco said.

Jaime struggled up and faced him, "You quit?"

"You don't quit," Marco said. "You just don't go back."

"And the bar? You're still gonna go to the bar, right?"

Marco smiled and wondered if Jaime could see his smile in the dark. "You wanna know something?" he said. "I hate going to bars. My mom used to pull me out of bed in the middle of the night to go into these beer joints to get my dad while she waited outside in the car." He paused. "Did you ever have to do that?"

"My dad drank at home."

"What? He didn't have any friends?"

Jaime missed the joke. "What are you going to do for money?" he asked.

"I thought about getting a real job."

"I thought this was as real as it got."

"A regular job then," Marco said. That was what he had told

Chris the afternoon they spent on the roof. He wanted a regular job and Chris offered to help him with a résumé. Instead of the dishwashing job he'd had back home, they wrote that he'd been a cashier. Instead of the cashier job he had in Houston, they noted assistant restaurant manager. Instead of the Office Procedures Certification he'd received from Houston Community College, which Chris had nagged him to take to leave the diner, they wrote Associates Degree in Business Administration. And rather than admit working as a burlesque dancer, they wrote that he managed the box office for an off-Broadway theater. He was afraid his work history would get checked out, that he would be stamped a fraud, but one place phoned him immediately and the manager hired him sight unseen because he liked his phone voice. It wasn't tele-marketing, the manager explained, but a good phone voice was still important. He started next week. Those words reverberated in his head until he heard himself say them. Jaime nearly jumped out of bed.

"You start next week?" he cried. "Where?"

"At an office in Midtown."

"How did you get a job this fast?"

"I don't know," Marco said, thinking a job this ordinary didn't need an explanation. If you wanted to work, it was there to take, and there was nothing mysterious about it. "I'm not picky, I guess, having worked at more unsavory establishments. I'll probably get fired as soon as they look at me."

"You didn't get an interview?"

"No. I got hired over the phone." Marco turned toward him. He looked, even in the failed light, or because of it, ready for another few drinks. "You're not happy I got the job?"

"I'm happy," he said. "It's just a shock. Why keep it a secret?"

"It wasn't a secret. I only started looking a few days ago." He pulled Jaime to him. "I just thought I would try something legit for a change. Maybe make some friends. Who knows."

"So you quit everything?"

"Pretty much," Marco said, though he hadn't worked out all the details. One thing firm in his mind was that he wouldn't go to the theater or the bar, but if Jean called him for a late-night dinner, he guessed he would still go. If he was short on cash, he figured he could always call Quentin. It wasn't like he even had to get naked for Quentin. A few smacks against the skull and he would have a good wad of cash. Marco pulled Jaime tighter against his chest. "I'm quitting everything but you," he said.

Marco stared into Jaime's eyes and then followed the drop of his nose and curve of his mouth, which was breaking into a smile. Marco wanted to say something, but then, without a hint of anything, Jaime told Marco he loved him. Marco felt his arms go limp, as if his body had been bled of emotion, when really, truly, Jaime's words had done nothing but fill him. He felt like a delicate vase stuffed with flowers, their perfume threatening to suffocate him with their overwhelming fragrance.

Marco didn't say anything. For so long he'd always heard those words as a way to prompt him for a response, a kind of springboard from which he was expected to leap out in a soaring expression of those same sentiments to whomever had said them first. Mostly it was the johns who made such claims, but for a long time before them it had been Chris. Tonight, however, he felt the words rise from his tongue like spontaneous hymns and they gathered at the roof of his mouth. The words were as delicate and pure as pale eucharists. Marco became Sunday School boy, making the signs of the cross, holy water and oil marking head, heart, and lips. He felt the heat of Jaime's breath evaporating his own, seizing it from out of his lungs and leaving him gasping, mouth dilating like that of a fish out of water.

Jaime lay under him, his face pressed hard against the pillow, moaning sweet sounds like a call to prayer. Marco came on bloodied knee, chest pounding under beating fists, fears burning away like incense. The sweet smoke coiled up as an offering to the waxed faces of the watchful saints and apostles and virgins. Jaime was the *milagro* arrived after years of petitions, of notebook scrawl and stark photo-booth photos of grief. Jaime was the broken limb now healed, crutch and cast abandoned, the safe return of what had gone missing, of the beloved who had set off to fight in some far-off sea. Marco never felt so ready to drown in his desire.

spring

t e n

The job was in an office building on West Fifty-fourth. The theater that televised *The Late Show* crouched at one end of the block, and the defunct Studio 54 on the other. A deli between them sold T-shirts for both. The New David All-Male Cinema showing double features of gay porn also sat on the block, across from a gallery of peep booths and a strip joint called Legs Diamond. Tour buses choked the street with exhaust fumes and their disgorged passengers crowded the sidewalks. The tourists never spoke a recognizable language. Then again, Marco never bothered to stop and listen to them. They might have just been suburban families from Delaware.

His first day at work, Marco hated the office, but persuaded himself to at least try it a while. Perhaps it never got any better than this cramped space with brown chairs on broken casters and gray carpet so frayed and worn that the tiles underneath poked out in places like dingy teeth in an ever-widening mouth. The desks were all pushed up against the walls and the walls were braced with shelves and the shelves were stacked with dusty boxes of letterhead with the old company logo, which Marco was instructed never to use or throw out. The single window, barricaded with burglar bars and chicken wire, was nailed shut. The only fresh air came from moving around the cluttered office. His throat felt sore by late morning and it nagged at him like a yellow sticky-note.

The company, called Stock Trade Publishing, did not actually publish anything. They sold newsletters written by supposed stock market experts, advertising them in the financial press, or on radio and television, and mailed out thousands of newsprint catalogs to previous customers or people who had the misfortune of being on the lists they bought from other companies. They sold newsletters and then sold the names of the people who had bought those newsletters to brokerage houses on Wall Street. It sounded illegal when Marco first realized the newsletters were a front to get the names. But he got used to it as the days passed, and by the end of the week the complaints became routine. Subscribers called about being harassed by brokers and brokers called to verbally piss on the leads the company had sold them.

Marco worked in the front office with Che and Irene. Both had recently graduated from Barnard and had tuition loans to pay off and apartments to keep. They always groaned about how exclusive Barnard had been, the hard work they had done, only to end up in a place like this. It made Marco feel better about never having earned a college degree.

Other than Che and Irene, three high school girls came late in the afternoons and worked until evening. All of them, including Irene, were Chinese. Che was a mix of Cuban and Thai. For a moment Marco wondered if his Asian looks had got him the job, but then he remembered he'd been hired over the phone. Besides, everyone seemed hopelessly straight. Che was about the only one who kept it interesting, telling Marco about a lesbian bar she sometimes went to with disappointing results. She never found anyone attractive or approachable. Marco didn't know if she was telling him about her near-lesbian moments because she wanted to show off, scandalizing the other employees, or to make Marco comfortable. Still, he liked her. She had the face of a glamour queen, smooth and pale-brown, plucked and lacquered without looking garish. She wore next to nothing except for patent leather thigh-high boots and short skirts. Against the cold, she draped a long faux leopard-print coat. She had a nose ring and a pierced navel. Irene, on the other hand, shopped from all-American mail order catalogs. She kept the catalogs on her desk and had the pastel, oversized sweaters and khakis delivered to the office. This was the one thing about the job he enjoyed—he wore whatever he liked, usually jeans and running shoes.

Even Lou, the office manager, whose name seemed more suited for a thug from Jersey than for a young Jewish guy, wore jeans and shirts creased as if he had recently torn them from the package. He had his own private office and only came out to pay the delivery boys who brought in his lunch. He was only twenty-three or so, like the rest of them, but he looked about ten years older. He had a receding hairline and always looked ready to fall asleep or not yet ready to wake up. He was the one who'd hired Marco, but Mr. Ehrenkratz, Lou's father, owned the business.

Mr. Ehrenkratz never came into the office. He called in every half hour to get a count on the number of orders placed after an ad ran in the papers. Che kept a running total so that she could give him an accurate count any time he asked for it.

No one did much work in the office. Marco passed his first week staring at the postcards Jean sent him from Nice and Bordeaux. When he got tired of his imaginary travels, of perhaps escaping to France with Jaime, he stared at the horoscopes he had pasted on the frame of his flickering computer screen. He used to hate the broad generalizations of the astrological forecasts published in one of the city's free weeklies, but lately the encapsulated messages were chillingly accurate. He couldn't let a week go by without getting the latest installment of what he should expect in his life. He needed that smudge of hope, any dull indication, no matter how vague, that his life with Jaime was not drying up as he suspected.

Che wrote frantic letters to the college boyfriend who had left her to study voodoo in New Orleans. He moved south after graduation and refused to give her a phone number. He said he didn't have one. She thought he was avoiding her and said so in the scrawled pages she sent him. Irene sat on the other side of the front office, near the postage meter machine, flipping through her catalogs. The salesmen worked in the cubicles in the back, and came into the front area on rare occasions, and then only to pass to the bathroom down the hall or out to the street to have a smoke.

Time seemed to collapse in that office. His second or third week there, each feeling like a month, Marco started taking Fridays off. He wanted to have an extra day on the weekends for Jaime because they weren't seeing much of each other. Jaime spent most of his nights at the bar and Marco was too tired from work to wait for him afterward. He also didn't want to smell the smoke in his clothes, the beer on his breath, or the musk of another man stamped onto Jaime's skin like a tattoo. The nights they did see each other, however, Marco sometimes felt too tired to have sex. He didn't know how much of this he should explain to Lou, but he didn't have to say anything because Lou pointed out that the office was more than covered. He reminded Marco of the high school girls who filled in on Friday, crowding the office with their gossip and teenage laments. Che had no problem at all with Marco taking time off. She had forgotten her troubles, the boyfriend in New Orleans, and became interested in a rich young guy who owned a film production company where she volunteered as a reader. She had worked for him as an intern while she was still at Barnard and now went to the young producer's apartment every few days to pick up scripts and have a quickie. Instead of the bright yellow legal pads on which she once wrote her free-verses of grief, she had thick film scripts and books on how to get love from men who loved too little.

"You never, ever, ever call them," Che advised, reading from her book.

"I never called Wilson," Irene added, distracted, bored. "When we were first dating, Wilson would always call me, until one time he asked why I never called him. My parents were really conservative, you know, and they told me, never call a man. They should always call you. They were pretty smart. Plus, I was really busy with school and I didn't have the time to call him. And also, I was kind of interested in someone else."

"Everyone should read this book," Che said, flipping through the book still in her hands. "Maybe I'll mail it to this guy I met last week. I gave him my phone number. I didn't think it was all that big of a deal because he was going back to the West Coast the next morning. He's been calling long distance ever since. Long distance. He called twice last night. First to ramble about how good it was to meet me and then a few hours later to apologize for calling so much. He finally got the point and said he wouldn't call until I called him."

Irene peeked from behind a mail-order catalog. "Are you?"

"No," Che said with an edge of resentment. "I like Holden." She seemed to think about him for a moment. "Should I call him? The book says I shouldn't. I should wait for him to call me, but I think that's only if we haven't had sex yet." She twisted the phone cord with her finger. "A few days ago, he said he really wanted to see me soon. And that was completely uninitiated."

"Oh, I say that to Wilson all the time," Irene said.

"But this was uninitiated," she fired back. "I hadn't said anything about wanting to see him. I mean, you tell Wilson you want to see him because he says he wants to see you, right?"

Irene shrugged and answered her ringing phone. Che pleaded with Marco. He didn't know what to say to put out the smoldering doubt threatening to engulf her. He did know one thing though: people only said they wanted to see each other to be polite, to make themselves out to be better than they were. He'd been feeling this about Jaime. Things had been good for a while, their lives stitching themselves together as fast and as unconscious as the knitting Marco saw one woman do on the train each morning. Only now Marco had reached some unscheduled stop and the finery that had been taking shape was now falling to pieces. He felt he was holding the end of a limp string and didn't know if Jaime was at the other end.

"Does that book say what men want?" Marco asked.

"Don't you know?" Che asked. "You're one of them."

He was one of them, but he had never studied men as Che had. He never bought books or read magazine articles about how to attract and keep them, how to give them the best sex they ever had, or, when it didn't work out, how to dump them without regret. Che seemed to know these things.

She rolled her chair closer to him, crossed her legs and almost took his hands in hers. "They want sex," she said.

"All of them?" He didn't know why he asked that. Of course they all wanted sex. He knew that more than anyone in the office, perhaps more than the writers of those books and how-to articles. He looked at Che who stared back at him as if he was her dumb brother.

"Of course they want sex," Che said.

"But you're talking about first dates."

"I'm talking first dates, boyfriends, brothers, uncles, fathers. I don't know one guy who hasn't wanted sex."

Marco thought of Jaime and how the sex used to carry him to Jaime's downtown apartment. Time hadn't passed that much for him to think back on it the way he did, feeling it with a heavy beat of nostalgia, but things had changed. The sex had begun to feel forced, and tiring, so that Marco lost his faith that their carnal pleasures would raise them to celestial heights. Their nights of defeated passion were like deconsecrated Last Suppers, feasts unworthy of even the most dismal take-out delis. Even after the sex, Marco was never left in peace. Jaime would keep nibbling at him during the night like a rat let loose on the spoils. And before starting his day, exhausted as he was, Jaime wouldn't let Marco get up to shower until they had sex again, sticky mouthed and sore as they were from the night before.

"You give it up on the first date," Che said to no one in particular, "and that's it. Second date, maybe they'll last a few weeks. The more you deny them that thing, that sex thing, the crazier they get for you. Then it's like a mathematical exponent. You might find yourself married and living happily ever after if you don't touch the guy until the honeymoon. Of course, I can never wait that long. I don't believe in holding back just to make a good impression. I'm sure half the idiots I've been with think I'm a whore. Fuck 'em."

eleven

Arriving at his subway stop after work, Marco got swallowed up into the maw of other riders, then coughed out onto the street. He slid down the icy sidewalk, trying to steady his feet on the concrete. His bad knee felt about as pained as the day he had injured it. He thought of nothing more than crawling into bed. The office and the stingy daylight hours left him wanting little else.

As he crossed West End Avenue, he spotted Sol getting out of her car. Under the dark sky of late afternoon, she looked dry and damaged, as if her entire being had suffered a bad dye job. A cigarette dangled from her crumpled mouth as she walked along the street. He hoped to get by without her catching sight of him. He didn't want to bother with her. He wanted to go to sleep and hope for a better tomorrow, but she called out to him just when he thought he had escaped.

"Kid! Where you been?"

"Whoring," he answered, thinking she would have said it anyway.

She didn't seem amused. The half circles under her eyes looked about as swollen as water balloons. Her mouth was without lipstick and chapped. He turned back to continue toward the apartment, but Sol wasn't finished.

"Don't bother going up," she cracked. "We got no heat an' no hot water."

"What happened?"

"Landlord shit, tha's all," she said, forcing a wad of phlegm into her throat, as if ready to spit out what choked her lungs. She changed the subject. "I think the bitch is playing me."

From her back pocket, she took out another cigarette without finishing the one in her mouth. Her head bobbed as if it might snap from her neck, her thoughts weighing her down, her eyes fat with grimy tears.

"I think she playing me," she said again, stabbing the cigarette between her pressed lips and pulling out a tattered book of matches from another pocket. She struck the one remaining light, but a sudden gust put it out, and she cursed, flinging the matchbook onto the street, searching her pockets for another. "You got a light?" She paused. "Lissen to me. You don't smoke." She went to her car and opened the door. "Get in," she said. "Get in before you freeze your skinny ass."

Marco did not want to get into the car, but whatever he could have said stalled out in his head, like a car that wouldn't start. He thought of his cold room, the frigid walls and bed sheets. What little energy he had was now extinguished. The passenger-side door fell open and Marco stumbled into the car, taking a lungful of fresh air first.

Sol punched open the sunroof—for his sake, he guessed. It was more than his father ever did when he lit up in the El Camino. Marco watched her waiting for the car lighter to pop back, for the coils to heat up, and when she lit her cigarette, she settled back in her seat and took a long drag. She kept her face turned away, as if engrossed by the cars going in and out of the parking garage across the street.

"You know how I know she playing me?" she asked, her breath fogging the window. "You know how I know?"

Marco didn't say anything. He didn't want to know.

"I don't," she said, exhaling slowly. "I just feel it. I feel like she be doin' that." Sol stuck her hand out, through the open sunroof, and flicked the ash off her cigarette. A few tears stained her pitted cheeks and her lips trembled when she turned back to look at the garage. "I don't know. Maybe I's just PMS-ing. Tha's what my friends say."

Marco didn't know if Sol was telling him about Bernice, who worked at the waste plant, or Yolanda, the one she had always been with, the one she broke up with and got back together with every few months. Sol had been playing both of them, but who played her, Marco didn't know.

"Well, you need to tell her something." Whoever she is, he thought. "Tell her how you feel."

"Think so?" She threw her cigarette out the sunroof and wiped her damp eyes. "I wanna call an' tell her, but wha's the point? Know what I'm saying?"

"At least she'll know how you feel."

"I guess."

Marco didn't know what he was talking about, and could have used Che's help, but Sol seemed calmed by it. She told him she would be up later. She just wanted to have another cigarette and thought she would spare him the suffocating smoke. The need to get away from her had somehow fortified him and he jumped out of the car and shot up into the apartment. She came up minutes later smelling like an ashtray and looking no better. She called one of them. Marco still didn't know who.

"No, you keep the key," she said into the phone. For some reason she was using the phone near his bedroom. Was she expecting his help? "I don't want the key back. Keep it. I don't want it. I said, I don't want it. I just wanna tell you no one else come in an' outta this apartment. Only you. Only you, *mami.*"

Marco slipped past her to the bathroom to brush his teeth. At the office, he had told Jaime on the phone, that he planned to come home and go to bed early. That was his excuse for not meeting with him after work, for putting it off until the weekend. Now with Sol shouting into the phone, he wanted to go somewhere, at least until her grief played itself out. He knew Jaime's place would be warm, the bed more comfortable, as Jaime liked to claim, his excuse for rarely spending the night at Marco's apartment. Still, the mere thought of the trains he would have to take to get downtown made him feel exhausted.

"Can you believe her?" Sol yelled from the living room. She came rushing to the bathroom door. "I say, Yolanda, I feel like a whore. You come in an' leave me, like a whore. Tha's what a whore is? Only for sex? An' she say she already has the perfect relationship, but she can't get no sex from it. An' tha's where I ask her if I'm just her whore. An' she say, if tha's how I feel about it, it's not her problem. Can you believe her? She calling me a whore. Tha's what she calling me. Right?"

She didn't wait for Marco to answer. She ran to her bedroom and slammed her door with a force meant to break it. She banged her windows and flung things around her room. Marco figured this must have been how his windows got cracked. As he sat on his bed, wondering what he should do now, he felt a draft shooting in through the cracks. He had made an effort to seal and caulk the windows, had even tacked weather-stripping around the frames, but none of it helped. The chill still bit, its fangs puncturing the layers of clothes he wore to bed each night. It was just too cold. He decided to head downtown.

He loaded his backpack with a change of clothes and turned off the lights. He would have been at the subway stop in minutes, if Sol hadn't been sitting on the living room couch, the television flickering and spilling soft colors against her damp face.

"Where you goin'?" she asked, her voice stripped to a whisper. "Not to that boy again. No one is that much fun."

Marco set his bag down and sat on the plastic garden chair that matched none of the other furniture in the room. Not the chrome shelving unit where the television sat or the scalloped-back purple couch where Sol sat.

"So, is it just him?" she asked.

"Yeah," he said. "I don't have energy for anyone else."

"You ain' Puerto Rican." She laughed. "Everything gets us hot. Gin, rain, money, whatever." Her laughter ended with a sharp grunt. "Tha's my problem I guess."

"I'm going to have some tea. You want some?"

"Is it gonna help me sleep?"

"It won't hurt."

"Whatever," she said as if picking a pubic hair from out of her mouth.

Marco set the water boiling in a pan without handles. It was the only clean pot in the kitchen. The others were filled with foamy grease and scraps of burnt food. Sol had left the pans to soak, as she put it, even though she'd warned him about leaving a mess since finding a mouse.

She came into the kitchen, tugging at the split ends in her bleached hair, and sat on the footstool by the window. She poked her fingers into the planter that held the dead impatiens. They'd withered to dry stubs. Nothing had helped them. Not even the Bustelo coffee grounds she had packed into the pot. She sighed, her breasts rising and falling back in heaps on either side of her belly, her thin legs jutting out from underneath. Marco couldn't believe she wasn't cold sitting by the window.

"You think it bad to want sex every night?" she asked, rolling a clot of dirt between her fingers. "I can't get it from that other one, Bernice. She just not into it."

"It's not bad," he said, thinking of his own situation, wondering if Jaime might give up on him and his weary excuses, and have sex with someone else, if he had not already done it. "It's not bad. But if she doesn't have the same drive you do, then it's gonna be a problem."

"I grew up with a mom an' dad who had sex every night. Even when they was scratching each other's eyes out, they was screwing. So a' course, I'm gonna want it. It's in the blood. I gotta have it. Tha's why I'm having all these problems. I have to get sneaky looking for it. If I had everything from one girl, I'd be okay."

"Where is she?"

"Yolanda or Bernice?"

"Bernice," Marco said, not knowing the difference.

"Home asleep or somethin'. She sleep half her life away. I know she got a tough job an' everything, but here I am, awake an' mad because she won't come over an' when she do, it's like she don't wanna touch me."

The water started boiling and Marco took an oven mitt and poured the water into two mugs. "Does she like sex?" he asked.

"I don't think so," she said. "She was abused as a child, you know, an' she got lots of problems. But I'm not a therapist. I'm her lover. I feel bad, you know, that she got abused an' everything, but I gotta get laid too."

Sol sipped her tea. Marco waited for his to cool, staring out the window at the glistening bricks on the next building. At one time, he had wanted sex a lot too. He used to spend ten dollars just to get through the door of a downtown sex club. A porn movie played upstairs, but most of the men lurked in the basement maze of suffocating cubicles, where they made it with one another under bare red bulbs. When the ten dollars seemed like too much of an investment, he dropped quarters into the peep booths in Times Square, a district forever flashing with possible, if fleeting, excitement. He couldn't remember when all his troubled desire had gone dry, when getting off seemed to get him nowhere, but he couldn't say he missed it. He wondered, though, if leaving that wholesale life was worth whatever respectability and security he thought he was winning with Jaime. The game he found himself playing felt as thin as a bingo card and about as interesting.

"Yolanda," Sol mumbled, her mouth sloppy with sleep, "we never had a good relationship, but we had great sex. With Bernice I got a good thing. She care about me. No one ever treated me that good. But I never had anyone fall asleep on me like she do."

After draining her cup, Sol went to bed and slept. Marco abandoned his plans to go downtown and went to his room but couldn't go to sleep. The cold kept him awake, so he sat on the floor, by the light of the lamp. He thought of plugging in the electric heater, but he was afraid the fuse would blow with the lamp still on, and in that moment, he felt more afraid of the dark than the cold. The light swept his wounded thoughts into the corners and under the bed where he didn't have to see them. He didn't want to recognize the infidelities Sol suffered, those he had suffered with Chris, those suffered by the male lovers and wives of the johns he knew. He didn't want to think he had played a role in these lies and deceit. He didn't want to think he might lose Jaime to the same terrible tragedy.

He followed the grooves of the floorboards and counted the crumpled pieces of paper he had neglected to throw out. Old numbers of the johns he once saw, and some, he had to admit now, he still saw to supplement his wages at the office. Leaving the business was harder than he had thought it would be. He hadn't realized how dependent he had been on the money and the men. Their desire for him, whether he believed them or not, was as important as the money. This was why he had returned to Chris so many times. Wasn't it? Chris's desire for him kept bringing him back. He wanted to feel wanted. Jaime was different. He was the first guy Marco ever desired. And for no good reason.

Marco called his voice mail to see if Jaime had left a final plea to get him downtown. If he had, he would have splurged on a cab to get there. There was no message. He called Jaime at home, but no one answered, not even the machine. He turned off the light and plugged in the electric heater. By the orange glow of the heated coils, he checked his shoes to make sure the battered scraps of paper with Jaime's name were still there. He would have taken them out and stuffed them into his socks, or even into the crotch of his underwear, if he had not been knocked into an immobile sleep as the first stroke of warmth rose from the heater.

twelve

At the office the following morning, between unanswered calls made to Jaime's apartment, Marco got an unexpected call from Chris. He needed a place to stay. Marco agreed to let him stay at his place. He was sure Sol wouldn't mind. They got along. But later, as Marco rode the subway home, it occurred he had agreed too quickly. He hoped Chris wouldn't stay for more than a night.

When Chris arrived, it was with the announcement that he had moved out of Seventeen. He came dragging most of his stuff behind him. They arranged what they could in Marco's bedroom and left the rest in the living room until after dinner. They returned with their stomachs aching from too much food and decided to leave everything else for later and got ready for bed.

Marco gave Chris the unused toothbrush he had been saving for Jaime. Marco used his own and wondered if the one Jaime had given him still stood in the mason jar, if Jaime ever used it himself, or if anyone else did.

Chris was already under the sheets when Marco returned to the bedroom. The blinds were open and Marco tried to pull them shut, but Chris rolled over and asked him to leave them alone. The moon was full and the light sifting through the window grates cut faint diamonds on the walls. Chris said they had an unearthly beauty. Marco warned him about the drafts.

"I'll keep you warm," Chris teased.

Marco groaned.

"I didn't mean sex," Chris said, getting up from the bed. "Christ, I'll go sleep in the living room if you want."

Marco apologized and pulled him back to bed. He spooned up behind Chris, his dick stiffening from the loose embrace. He hoped Chris didn't think he meant anything by it. He hadn't curled up with anyone in a while. He and Jaime had been working too much and spending too little time with each other. But even making love to one another had dried up. It was not as tender as before. The last time they'd had sex (and Marco could not and would not let himself remember when that was), Jaime seemed frantic, inhaling poppers, moaning into the small amber bottle, almost forgetting Marco was there. The poppers made Marco feel as if he weren't enough. Jaime's need for sex, his blind scratch for it, left Marco numb and disgusted. He wanted Jaime to want him, as he had before, not the way he did now, which reminded him of the desperation of the johns. Despite all that, however, he still wished the body next to him was Jaime instead of Chris.

"You going to miss me?" Chris whispered.

"Sure," Marco said.

"Try it again," Chris said and yawned. "Try it with feeling."

"I meant it the first time."

"I guess I should say I'm gonna miss you too, but I won't because I've been missing you for so long already, now I only get this really tired feeling when I think about leaving."

"Do we have to fight?"

"Who's fighting?" Chris yawned again. "I'm not fighting."

Marco felt a pain flare in his neck. The muscles in his shoulders jerked, sending another jabbing pain. He begged Chris for a massage and directed him to the bottle of oil in the junk drawer, then to the

146

constellation of pain breaking across his back. Chris kneaded his stiff shoulders. The relief turned back the clocks. They were in their old apartment in Houston. Nothing had changed. Jaime didn't exist.

"So are you going to tell me about the boy?" Chris slapped the words down like he did his hands against Marco's knotted neck.

"What boy?" Marco asked.

"The one in the photos."

"I thought I took that down," Marco mumbled to himself.

"Too late. I saw him already."

"It wasn't so you wouldn't see him."

"I forgot, you're not as sensitive about those things as I am."

"Like you took a vow of chastity after our breakup," Marco said.

Chris's hard jabs were providing less and less relief, but Chris didn't seem to notice and continued pushing his knuckles into Marco's back. Marco let him continue, but he couldn't help think how tired he was of having Chris tell him who he was, what he was capable of doing. Or not doing. Which seemed to be his point most of the time. Marco wanted to say, for himself, who he was, what he stood for. He wanted to own himself, or at least keep a part of himself that Chris couldn't get to, and Jaime seemed to be the one thing on which Chris had no hold. Chris didn't know him, and never would, if Marco could help it.

"He's a guy," Marco said. "That's all."

"He knows about your sordid past?"

"Yeah, but he's a working boy too."

"I thought they weren't your type."

"He's different," Marco said.

Chris stopped massaging Marco's shoulders and rolled into the tight space beside him. To Marco, the massage didn't feel finished. Chris had always worked his entire body from the back of his neck to his feet. He guessed the sudden stop had to be about Jaime, but he was too sleepy to ask. Besides, he didn't feel as if he had said anything untrue. Jaime was different. He loved Jaime and didn't want to dilute his feelings. But where was he tonight? In what hotel room or apartment? In who's arms?

"He's cute," Chris said. He reached up to snatch the photos off the vanity. He looked at them in the faint light. "What's he like?"

"What do you mean, what's he like?" Marco asked, pulling the photos from his hands. He looked at himself in the black and white frames of the photos. What possibilities and excitement he felt then! He'd never thought he would be capable of feeling anything. Chris had always told him he wouldn't and had almost convinced him of it.

Chris propped himself on an elbow. "I've always told you everything."

"And sometimes I wished you hadn't."

"Forget it," Chris said, rolling over so that his back was to Marco. "I'm not going to beg."

"I'm just curious about what you're going to do."

"What am I going to do? Run it through the zipper in Times Square?"

"It just makes me nervous to talk about him," Marco said. "Talking about it always ruins it." His mother used to warn him never to talk about the really good things in his life, the things that made him happy, the dreams he dreamed. He had to keep them to himself or risk the possibility of having jealous people tear them away from him. What did his mother dream? What did Jaime?

"You like the guy?" Chris asked.

"I think I love him," Marco whispered.

He felt guilty for a moment. He'd never told Chris he loved him unless prompted. He expected Chris to say something, but when he didn't, Marco thought he should keep his own mouth shut.

"He's Chinese?" Chris asked.

"Filipino."

"So you have an Asian thing?"

"One guy is not a thing," Marco defended and pushed Chris away.

"I only dated Latin boys because they weren't cut. It wasn't necessarily the Latin thing. I only wanted them because they were uncircumcised. I still mourn the loss of my foreskin."

"So get it reconstructed," Marco shot back, annoyed by his pathetic explanation to justify the string of guys he dated. They all looked the same and Marco never knew if he looked like them or they like him. Who came first?

148

Chris rolled onto his back. "You know, there is a device I saw advertised in the back of a porn magazine that supposedly stretches the skin over time. It looked painful, but it might be worth it because a naked body with a flaccid, uncut penis is so beautiful. It's that classic David thing. It just looks right. That little encasing ready to be opened."

"Little?" Marco pretended to be insulted.

"Smaller is sometimes better. It's an asset to not be overendowed like you." He sounded like a scientist explaining the mating preferences of the gay male species. "And yes, once you open the little encasing, it's like, oh my god, look what's inside. Whereas a cut cock is just like a wound. It's just hanging there like scrap meat." Chris yawned. "Do you have a foreskin? I don't remember."

"You don't remember," Marco said, trying not to sound put down by the improbable question and its hateful implication. There was no way Chris could have forgotten. He was just being bitchy. "I was the contestant you kept calling back for another interview because you couldn't decide if I had one or not and was disqualified because I only had, like, half a foreskin."

"Oh, yeah," Chris stammered with a suppressed laugh. "Now I remember. The skin never covers the head. "

"It does," he defended. "When it's cold."

"Once a year, on a cold winter's night, it might cover the head, but never when you're hard."

"No, it never completely covers the head when I'm hard." For a moment, Marco imagined that their conspiratorial whisperings of sex might have been what happened at the adolescent sleepovers he had never been allowed to go to, his father claiming they were only for *viejas*. Marco nudged Chris. "Hey, are you playing with yourself? Is that why you're asking me these questions?"

"No," Chris said, falling back to a near-sleep monotone. "I just never thought you had much of a foreskin. Yeah, you had a little extra, which was nice, but when you have a lot, it's so much nicer." He yawned, his arm falling over Marco's chest. "It's nice to masturbate boys with a foreskin. If you're cut, you get all that chafing. It's one of the bigger tragedies of my life."

"Before meeting me, right?"

Chris burst out laughing. Marco knew he would. It was why he said it. Chris laughed hard enough to shake the bed. Sol shouted at them to shut up and go to sleep. Her shouting did nothing more than make Chris laugh harder, pushing him into a fit of convulsions. The silly storm passed though and only the deep guttural rumblings remained. Chris sighed, regaining his breath, composing himself. He turned to Marco and Marco took in his face, which, despite the dark, seemed threatened by another storm. His eyes glistened at the corners and his mouth seemed to break and turn down into a pained arc. Marco pulled Chris close. They didn't speak, but Marco knew what Chris was thinking. He had the same thoughts. What lives they had lived.

"You know," Chris said, his voice almost smothered by sadness and the late hour, "you're my first love. And I'm never going to have that again. Neither of us can go back to that place when we didn't know anything, when we were just beginning to explore what it meant to be with another person. It's never going to be the same. Ever. Not with anyone." He pulled Marco against him. The heat of their bodies drew them closer to the darkness of sleep. "Every time we got back together, I had this hope that we'd stay together. I know we joked about calling each other in five years, or something like that, but I believed it. If it didn't work out now, maybe it could later. But I don't think that anymore. We can't go back. I don't want to. I don't want to be that fat, overbearing, unfaithful, queen."

"And I don't want to be that thick-headed—"

"Insular," Chris added.

"Insular," Marco repeated. Chris liked calling him insular. Marco doubted he would have known the word otherwise. "I was so pathetic."

"Well, you can't expect much from a Mexican dishwasher," Chris said, kissing his cheek.

"Cashier," Marco corrected. "I was a cashier when you met me."

He had only mentioned the dishwashing job once, a part-time job he had in high school, but Chris seemed to memorize nothing but the stupid details, the dismal stations Marco held, his failed attempts to move past them. He had tried—and he was growing tired of having to point it out, even if it was only to himself—but he had tried to give Chris what he wanted, to make up for past mistakes. Perhaps he saw through it and realized that they were only disassociated motions, chaste kisses, chill hands surrendered under restaurant tables, while his heart remained locked away, waiting for someone else. Chris didn't want to be pleased. He wanted to be loved in the way that Marco loved Jaime.

"Does this new boy of yours make you happy?" Chris asked.

"I don't want to talk about him," Marco said.

"Well, I do," Chris insisted, the timbre of coming sleep ringing his words. "Does he make you feel good?"

"I guess. I don't know. I don't think it's going to work out." Marco said it more for Chris than for himself. He brought the sheet up to his mouth and bit the edge. The fabric was still rough and smelled new. There was no scent of Jaime anywhere. "We were supposed to see each other this weekend, but then he took a spot at the theater."

"So go see him after the show."

"I can't. You know that."

"Oh," Chris groaned. "You and your stupid rules."

"They're not anymore stupid than yours."

Chris didn't say anything.

"I'm just hoping he quits soon," Marco added.

"You quitting too?"

"I have quit. Don't say you forgot this either. You helped me with the résumé." Marco turned to him. "Your memory is shot."

"I must be talking in my sleep. I don't even know what I'm asking." He yawned. "So you quit everything, huh? Even Quentin?"

"Everything," Marco said, trying to convince himself of it.

"How much did you make off him anyway?"

"Please, don't bring him up."

"You know," Chris said, "I never saw a cent from that referral."

"And you're not going to. If you want, I'll buy dinner again tomorrow, but that's it."

"That's it?" he whined.

"Yeah, that's it," Marco said and brought the sheet over his head.

"All right, already," Chris said and turned away.

Marco lay covered by his sheets. He felt as far from sleep as from the paradise he wanted to flee to with Jaime, places he had been clipping from travel magazines and kept in his junk drawer.

"I read about this great coastal village on the Pacific near Guatemala," he said, his breath trapped by the sheet against his face. He felt he was floating in the warm harbor of his dream. "I want to go and live there a few months."

"You have the money?" Chris challenged.

"I've been saving."

"Enough to stay there a few months?"

"A few. I just want to get out of here."

thirteen

While Chris spent the following night at Nathan's, Marco spent his at home, listening to the stereo in the living room. He woke up early the next morning, in his bed, alone. He got up and checked his voice mail. Jaime hadn't called yet. Or anyone. He wanted to call Jaime, but he didn't know where to reach him, where he might have spent the night. Jaime had promised to call with the hotel and room number, but then, he'd only promised.

Marco got dressed and went out. The snow had piled up during the night, and it depressed him because as beautiful as it was, this was supposed to be spring. Where were the buds on the trees? The shoots breaking ground? He felt suffocated by his layers of clothes and the packed thoughts that kept him from seeing the unadulterated snow as anything more than drudgery for shovels and plows. The cars parked along the street were almost buried. The snow banked to the top of the tires. All the storefronts on Broadway were shuttered and closed, which was fine with Marco since he didn't know where he wanted to go. He once thought hustling would buy him the time to do what it was he wanted to do. (Which was . . .) But the time had only made him restless, as it did this morning.

The neon sign of the Key West Diner glowed across the street. He didn't want to go there. The pink walls and aquamarine vinyl booths made him nauseous. They were the same cheap colors of the houses in his *colonia.* One of the waiters at the diner, a Mexican, also insisted on speaking to him in Spanish. The conversations always left him feeling stupid. He only went there when he'd exhausted every other possibility for a meal. He was glad he wasn't hungry yet.

He thought of heading to the bookstore to read the travel magazines, but it wouldn't be open yet. He had to find something to do other than sit in the living room and listen to the stereo again. All the songs were terribly sad. At least they were last night. He'd been listening to one station, after leaving a message with Jaime's roommate, hoping Jaime would get it so that Marco could join him after his last dance. He was willing to suspend his rules, even if they pushed him toward irrationality, which was perhaps what love, a stalled love, needed. But Jaime never called back and the songs just kept rolling out of the stereo like damp toilet paper. Marco fell asleep on the living room couch and woke up in his own bedroom. He assumed Chris had carried him to bed, but Chris had not returned from Nathan's. It could have been Sol, but he couldn't imagine her lifting him, even with the help of one of her women.

He stopped at a corner *bodega* and picked up the Sunday paper and a cup of coffee and started home. Heading back down the street, he tried to shrug off the morning, its emptiness and near desperation. Usually at that hour, when he went running, the delivery trucks lined up along the street, unloading pallets of fresh bread and boxes of fruits and vegetables. On weekdays, a brigade of sleepy children marched down to the school, their parents following behind until they reached the front steps.

At the corner, Marco gulped down his coffee, waiting for the light to change. He didn't have to wait, since only a few cabs plowed through the snow-choked streets, but he also didn't want to return home. He decided then to turn around and trudge to Central Park.

He arrived at the reservoir in good time, despite the cold and the dead weight of the paper. He leaned against the fence, clutching it with a free hand, his gloved fingers poking through the chain-link. His knee throbbed with a slight, warm ache. He wondered when he might ever get back to his running. He was surprised he wasn't dead yet—he always thought he would die if he didn't run. He believed this so much he ran in all kinds of weather.

Last year, when the snow got so high and thick that it was impossible to maneuver over the sidewalks, and most everyone walked the plowed streets, in danger of being run over by the cabs and buses sliding over the slush, he came out to the track and ran the trench that had been cut through the knee-high snow. He was the sole runner those mornings, and on other mornings when the threat of some coming storm blotted out the Midtown buildings. He never gave up. He ran his laps and returned to the basketball courts near the apartment building, walking the perimeter of the blacktop, shaking out his legs, cooling his body and repeating to himself the motto stuck onto the basketball backboard that read: *Winners Never Quit*. It was paid advertising from an athletic shoe store, the phrase something of a cliché, but it got him running.

The mornings he didn't feel like going out he would think of that backboard and gently persuade himself to slip on his shorts, his shoes, see how that felt. Did he still not want to run? He'd lead himself out of his room and down to the street. How did he feel now? Soon he'd find himself sprinting up the street, filling his lungs with the raw air of the waking city, the smell of coffee brewing in the corner *bodegas*. He knew who he was then and felt himself in his body.

Leaning against the fence this snowy morning, he felt some of himself come back to him, his body remembering itself. He felt his body notice something—the way a person living in the city always seemed to be aware of their surroundings, the perhiphery, fearing the murderous cabs, the bike messengers and delivery boys streaking through intersections, the bundled incoherence of blathering men rocking themselves in the corner of subway cars—and Marco jumped, his heart quickening, sweat pouring out under his arms. It was another runner. Another? Was he still a runner? It had been months since he set foot on the track, but he guessed he still considered himself a runner, though he reminded himself it was never just about the running. Some days he felt he was indeed saving his life, from getting beat by the world, this city, his father way back when.

Los Chamacos weren't playing as much. Some of the members complained that their *viejas* thought they spent too much time gigging and not enough time at home. Also, the music had dropped in popularity. They continued to use traditional accordions and trumpets while all the other bands had begun to use synthesizers and other electronic instruments. Marco's father had refused to play one of those huge electronic keyboards. He claimed they had no soul and insisted that a real maraca sounded better than a canned copy. He wanted to continue with tradition and even refused to eat in Mexican restaurants where sad-looking old men hit keyboards like chimpanzes. His father said the songs were already programmed into the machine like a jukebox. If anything, they just sat in a tinseled corner and sang, if you could call it singing.

Yet Marco's father wasn't even doing that. He was home a lot, sleeping through the afternoons, recovering from the late nights of drinking more and playing less. Everyone tiptoed around the house making as little noise as possible.

One weekend, when money was as tight as a belt on a fat man, Marco's mother refused to drop him and his brothers and sisters off at the movie theater, as she sometimes did, to keep them out of trouble with their father. *Las cuatas* went next door, to gossip with the neighbors, and *negro* went across the field to the other *colonia*. Marco stayed home because none of those domestic adventures interested him. He was twelve or thirteen, the age when everything, on whatever day, seemed boring. Nothing was big enough, everything was as he knew it, and what he knew was that he was stuck in a nowhere place with nothing.

He turned on the radio, hoping to find a call-in contest for movie tickets, but whoever had used the radio before him had left it *á todo vuelo,* as his mother liked to say. So, when he turned it on, the music blasted, and his father shot out of bed without even putting on his pants. Marco was so scared he ran out of the house, not bothering to turn off the radio. The music was loud enough to make the neighbors on either side come out of their houses to see what was happening. Marco stood, first on the porch, then in the yard because his father came outside, his skinny, hairless legs glaring in the light of the late afternoon sun. He had a belt in his hands and didn't seem to notice everyone watching him, practically naked, stepping into the yard. Marco fled to the mailbox, not knowing where to go next. *No corres y ven pa'ca.* His father's insistence that he return was as inviting as a cold tortilla. Marco shook his head no. His father's eyes seemed to open for the first time but just as soon returned to slits from the light. Marco said nothing and stumbled backward onto the road.

His father's words kept repeating themselves in his head. *No corres, no corres, no corres.* It meant "don't run," but the last word sounded like *corrido,* the name of those songs Los Chamacos played. They were tragic songs that people danced in a quick trot. It was a kind of run. Marco wondered if his father was talking in his sleep, mourning the band, their songs.

His father lurched forward and his lips tightened into a grim line. He must have sensed the neighbors because his body shuddered, as if from a chill, and his feet curled into themselves as if he had stepped into a patch of spiny *cadillos.* Marco knew he would be blamed, but instead of waiting for the punishment, he got ready to run. *No corres,* his father said again. *No corres o te va doler más.* His father didn't say more. He didn't have to.

Marco jumped onto the road and ran, leaving his father in the yard like an obscene lawn ornament. He shot past the neighbors still outside and then the next couple houses, boarded up because the people were up north *en la pisca.* He passed Doña Petra's house without stopping. She usually asked him about his family, but that afternoon, he had no time for her or anyone else who might have been out tending their dusty little plots. He made it to the edge of the highway where the cars bulleted by and a large semi-truck screeched past. His heart beat so fast, his lips trembling, that he didn't signal the truck driver to blow his horn as he and his brother liked to do.

Marco stood there, not knowing if he should risk crossing the two lanes to get to the other side, where it seemed safer. He looked back to see if his father had jumped into his El Camino to come after him, but the road sat empty, its *caliche* dust untroubled. A pain flowered in his gut and he doubled over with a cramp. He started crying, not about what had happened, but about what would when he got home. That wait seemed more terrible. He wiped his eyes and headed toward Mister G's, the corner grocery where he caught the schoolbus every morning. They had video games there, and he thought he might find a quarter in one of the machines, abandoned by someone who could afford not to care about the small change.

He left that place, that clot of dirt where he grew up. He left his parents, his sisters, his brother. He sent them postcards once in a while to tell them he was still alive, which he guessed he did out of spite because growing up he was convinced they would have squeezed the life out of him if he had let them. If he had not run, he had no doubt it would have happened. He had one of those childhoods that would have won him a spot on a tell-all talk show if he cared to confess every horrible detail. Which he didn't. He simply wanted to forget it. As soon as he graduated high school, he counted up the money he had saved from his restaurant job and moved to Houston because it was farther away than San Antonio or Austin. It was a full six-hour drive.

When he got back to the apartment, Chris not yet back, Marco slumped on his bed and started reading the paper. He felt as pathetic as those people who spent their Sunday reading the paper because they had nothing better to do. He went through the front page and the city and arts sections before he realized he was doing nothing more than flipping through the pages and not reading at all. He could not read. The words looked unintelligible. The printed letters may as well have been Chinese characters or glyphs of a now-forgotten language.

He decided to call his machine again. The service clicked on. One message. In a congested, hoarse voice, Jaime asked Marco to meet him at the Paramount Hotel lobby at two o'clock. Marco played the message again to bring Jaime's face to mind. He wanted to see Jaime that instant, but the clock only marked ten. Too late to be early and too early to be late, he didn't know what he would do to fill the hours. He didn't want to read any more of the paper. So he set his alarm clock and went to sleep.

At the hotel, he felt unsettled by the grand lobby, its gray carpet and opalescent lighting, the overstuffed eggplant-purple couches and the rich wood tables with the heavy black phones, which seemed to weigh about ten pounds each. The stairs, with their glass-paneled banister, rose against a brushed metal wall up to a dim mezzanine. He stayed on the ground floor, sitting in one of the plush couches, where Jaime had asked him to wait. He expected Jaime to walk in any moment.

Fifteen minutes passed and Jaime did not come. Marco became restless. He knew Jaime would show, but being in the hotel bothered him, with its lustrous and lurid quiet. He stepped over to the kiosk where a thin Asian guy stood behind the counter. Supposedly, the hotel only hired actors and models. They worked part-time as doormen, at the front desk, and, by the gorgeous looks of the guy at the kiosk, selling magazines and postcards. Marco was about to ask the guy if he was a model or an actor, if the rumor about the hotel employees was true, when he felt Jaime's breath against his ear.

"Sorry about the wait," he whispered.

When Marco turned to hug him, he noticed Jaime's wet hair and felt the dampness of his face. He smelled of anonymous hotel soap. Marco couldn't imagine that Jaime had come in from the cold since he also wasn't wearing a coat.

"I wanted to look good for you," Jaime said, biting his lip.

"So, you have a room here?" Marco asked, forcing the words out.

"Sort of."

Marco nodded. He didn't think he could utter another word. His throat felt caked with jealousy. "You're sharing it with another guy from the theater?"

"No."

"Then it must have been a damned good weekend."

"It's nice, huh?"

"It's sickening."

"You don't like it?"

"I love it," Marco said.

"I love it too." Jaime stepped back, taking in the lobby, as if he hadn't already seen it before. "I never knew this kind of place was just around the corner from the theater. It's like the two extremes. On Broadway are the naked boys and the Howard Johnson. This side has the hotel with the velvet couches. Have you been in one of the rooms?"

"Once or twice," Marco said. He had been there once, when Chris had shared a room with Franklin, the Taiwanese gymnast Chris was dating at the time. Their invitation to see the room, and Marco's resulting jealousy, was a kind of Chinese torture. "Are you going to take me up?"

The room itself was no bigger than a closet. The bed, which took up most of the space, looked like a flattened cloud. The comforter and pillows were stuffed with feathers that scratched at the back of Marco's neck when he lay against them. On the wall behind the bed, a huge silk-screen of an oil painting towered. Jaime started talking about the woman in the painting, but Marco's eyes were still taking in the rest of the room: the small bedside table and the light encased in a thin tube suspended from the ceiling; the bright metal chair; the raw wood armoire fitted with a television. The bathroom door was open and out spilled a black and white tiled floor, a brushed steel basin shaped into an inverted cone, and a clear plastic shower curtain beaded with water.

"And you didn't invite me sooner?" Marco interrupted whatever Jaime had been saying about the painting. "I can't believe you didn't call."

Jaime lay on the bed and traced the shape of Marco's neck. "You know how it is after a show. Naked bodies are the last thing I want to see."

Marco sensed the light sarcasm, but it didn't matter. They were together now. "I was thinking we should forget the rules for a while. I haven't seen enough of you."

Jaime leaned over and kissed him. He rubbed Marco's crotch with his hand and began unbuttoning his pants. Marco felt himself go as thin and mute as a paper doll. He felt helpless as Jaime continued to undress him. He didn't want to have sex right then. Not in that hotel room. He asked Jaime to stop, but he didn't seem to listen.

"Please," Marco said, louder. "Stop it."

"C'mon," Jaime whined.

"No," Marco said, pulling up his underwear and jeans. "I don't want to have sex where you've done other men."

"I'll change the sheets."

"It's more than that." He buckled his belt.

"So we'll do it in the shower." Jaime reached for Marco. "Take your clothes off."

"This is all you want? Isn't it?" Marco felt a tightness clutch his face. He had begun to believe the girls at the office, what they had been saying about men, and suspected that sex was all Jaime wanted.

"It's just that I haven't seen you in a while."

"So why can't you just be with me?" Marco pulled away and paced the room. "Why does it have to be about sex all the time?"

"When I think of you I think of sex."

It should have made Marco feel wanted, but it didn't.

"All right," Marco said, forcing his pants open and grabbing his crotch. "Let's go. You want this, don't you?" He pulled his dick out and it grew stiffer than it had in weeks. "Let's get this over with."

He hoped Jaime would see that his wanting him made him feel cheap, unwanted even, but Jaime had a dumb expression on his face, as if he couldn't believe his luck. Jaime pulled his own pants down and had Marco penetrate him. Marco didn't feel anything throughout and couldn't come. He rolled over and lay on the bed when he felt he had done enough. Jaime got up and took a quick shower.

161

"C'mon," he said, stepping from the bathroom, a towel wrapped around his waist. "Let's get out of here. We'll go to my place."

"I want to lie here." Marco sighed. "We need to talk."

"We'll talk at my place," he offered.

"What's wrong with talking here? You paid for the room. Right?"

"Not exactly," Jaime said. He swallowed hard and blinked. "The room belongs to this guy I met at the theater."

"A dancer?" Marco asked. His throat felt stuffed with a bar of soap. He repeated, though he did not know how, "A dancer?"

"A john," Jaime said.

Marco got up from the bed and crossed to the bathroom door. It was one thing to do a john in an hour and another to spend an entire night with him in his hotel room. Still, Marco didn't know what to think. He leaned against the door frame as if preparing for disaster. He looked at Jaime, at his dark hair dripping and dark eyes blinking as if to clear a mote trapped in them.

"This john," Marco asked, "where is he?"

"I told him to take a walk. I told him you were coming."

"Oh, he knows about me?"

"I told him about you." Jaime's mouth twisted into a smile.

"You told him about me," Marco repeated. "And he approves?"

"Don't make it harder than it is," Jaime said, raising his voice.

"What should I say?" Marco asked, bringing his voice up to Jaime's, as if to match a wager on a street game of cards. "What am I supposed to think?"

"I don't know." Jaime backed down. "He's just business."

"You met him at the theater," Marco said, and Jaime nodded. "And then?"

"And then what?"

"You came here?"

"What? Am I supposed to explain everything that happened?" Jaime paused and fixed his towel. "I met him at the theater Friday night. We came back here. He gave me his number here at the hotel in case I wanted to come back after the show. I told him no, of course, because I thought I would get a room at the Carter, but I didn't get any other business and the snow was bad and the theater was empty."

"Why didn't you call me?"

"I'm not supposed to, remember?"

"You couldn't go home?"

"There weren't any cabs."

Marco felt tempted to ask why he didn't take the train, but he figured there was an excuse for that too, and what was the point anyway? Jaime had not gone home. There was no way of changing that. Last night had ended and what remained was this frayed and frantic morning. "So you called the guy up and he was happy to hear from you."

"Yes," Jaime said indignantly.

"Did you at least get another one-fifty?"

"It wasn't like that. He nearly got another room for himself."

"Oh, not only rich, but a gentleman, too." Marco shifted his weight. His bones pressed against the door frame.

"You don't know anything," Jaime mumbled.

"Well you know he's in love with you."

"You don't know that."

"They always fall stupid in love or get delusional," Marco shouted.

"The guy just wants to spend a few days with me." The words came loud, bulleting from between clenched teeth. "That's all. Then he flies back to Belgium."

"You flying back with him?"

"I wish I was," Jaime answered with a defeated laugh. "You are making this so difficult. What's happened to you? Have you forgotten that this is just business? It's only a few days. I could make a lot of money. We could go somewhere."

Marco remained by the door. He felt unhinged and out of place. If he belonged anywhere it was in the dingy rooms of the Carter. Not here. Not in a room with a subdued lavishness that made him feel filthy. But Jaime was here, and Marco, not knowing what to say, but knowing what he felt, afraid it would all end soon, crossed toward Jaime and kissed him and kissed him until they lay on the bed. Jaime spoke first. He sounded exhausted.

"Why," he asked, "does it feel like I'm asking your permission?"

"Because I'm your boyfriend," Marco replied, tracing Jaime's beauty mark with his finger. "You're asking me because I'm your boyfriend."

Jaime nodded with hesitant jerks. "This john isn't anybody."

"He might not be anybody right now, but sometimes at the end of the little romance, before they fly back to wherever they come from, they give you so many little trinkets and promise so many things, you think, maybe. Maybe you could be with them."

Jaime sneered. "I'm not in a little romance."

Marco flashed him a smile. He knew what it was like. He'd stayed at the nice hotels and eaten at the good restaurants. The johns spent a lot of money on him. He believed them, like maybe they really liked him, thought he was worth knowing, as one john said, but then a few weeks later, they'd hire out the next dancer in the lineup.

They had a late lunch at the noodle shop where they had gone the night they met (Jaime didn't order anything because he had already had lunch) and then they went downtown to Jaime's apartment. Out of habit, they tried to have sex again, but Marco was too busy hating the john to get turned on and Jaime couldn't come. It didn't matter. Marco just wanted to hold Jaime and would have held him all night if Jaime hadn't said he needed to get back to the hotel. Needed to get back? *Needed?* Marco hated that Jaime had used the word. Why couldn't he call the john and tell him that he needed to spend the night with his boyfriend instead? He needed Jaime and he hated that he needed Jaime more than Jaime needed him.

f●urteen

When Marco got home from work, Sol had not arrived yet, and Chris, who had already lived there a week, was somewhere else too, supposedly arranging the departure that never seemed to come. Marco sat in his room, the walls echoing with the sounds of laughter and radios from the neighboring apartments. He wished someone would come to the door to tell him he wasn't the fool he felt he was. Jaime hadn't called in days. He wondered if he was still in the country or if he had pulled out his passport and flown to Belgium with his john. Marco rolled onto his side and tried to picture what Belgium was like. He gave up his tortured dreaming when Sol came home in a loud crash only to go back out again for a date with one of her women. Chris came soon after, talking about the possibility of moving to the West Coast. Marco offered a stillborn excitement.

The days moved on and away from him, one right after the other, without so much as a break to signify them. Then he got a phone call at the office one afternoon and Chris's voice focused his mind. He said he was calling to say good-bye. Marco did not say anything and Chris asked if he was still on the line. Marco said yes and looked at the clock, branding the hour into his memory as the last time he might ever hear this voice because Chris admitted that though he'd bought a bus ticket to L.A., he didn't know if he would stay there or keep moving. He wouldn't say any more. Marco offered to meet him at the Port Authority bus station, but Chris refused. In those last minutes Chris made no promises to write or call or otherwise keep in touch.

When they hung up, Marco grabbed the men's room key and went down the hall to lock himself in a bathroom stall. He started whimpering as he sat down. He didn't bother laying any toilet paper onto the seat. His ass felt cold. He thought about taking a cab down to the station, but he had spent most of his pocket money at lunch. He thought about calling Chris back (but how to reach him at the bus station? would they page him?) to tell him he was coming with him. He'd leave everything too. But maybe Chris had it right, finally. He might have wanted to undo his past by not bringing it with him. That included Marco.

Tears slid down his face. He couldn't believe they had ended it, the years of knowing each other, in a couple of minutes over the phone, and now he was crying about it in a bathroom stall. He wiped his face with the rough toilet paper and sat looking at the damp wad in his hands. He knew Chris had loved him, had saved him, taught him to give himself up to love. Chris had patiently given himself over when Marco didn't know what that meant. He couldn't have done that for anyone, including himself.

Marco arrived home from work and went to his room. He curled up in bed and stared at the door to the closet where he kept his clothes and the suitcase he had brought to New York. In the suitcase, he kept the clothes he rarely wore. The clothes he liked he kept on hangers and in the bureau. A few of the drawers were open. A lazy anger banged in his chest; he hoped Chris had not taken his clean socks.

He got up to see what was missing, but everything seemed to

be there, only picked through, which he had probably done himself that morning or the morning before that. He had stopped paying attention to what he did anymore. He pushed the drawers closed, including the junk drawer, without giving it another glance.

It had been a while since he had gone through the vagabond pile of articles he'd been cutting from travel magazines. A little more than five months had passed since he started saving for his big escape. When he had initially gone over it in his head, he didn't think it would take more than two months to get enough money together. And though Jaime kept saying he liked the idea, Marco now knew Jaime had never intended to go anywhere with him. He hadn't even bothered calling since they saw one another at the Paramount a week ago. The john should have only been a few days. Where was Jaime now?

The strip of photos lay on the vanity. Marco and Jaime had taken turns sitting on each other's laps, which, despite the short curtains of the booth, made them vulnerable to all the roughnecks at the arcade. The flash bulbs popped and captured a burgeoning happiness he would have fought to defend that night. He had enough strength then to take the whole bad place down. Tonight, alone in his room, he didn't even have the courage to look at the photos. Jaime had punched the air out of him. He didn't have the breath to say he loved anyone. Jaime was the first and last. Marco had seen himself reflected in Jaime's dark eyes. All he had now was a stark strip of photos. He folded them up, ready to drop them into the junk drawer, but then he had an idea.

He grabbed a garbage bag and began putting all the odd scraps lying around in his room, then the clothes he rarely wore or didn't fit him. He pulled out his suitcase and emptied it of all the ripped socks and baggy underwear. He threw away the pair of salmon-colored briefs Chris had bought him for his first night at the theater. He threw away everything that reminded him of the theater or the city.

When he got to the bureau he suddenly stopped cold. The familiar fear about his money clutched at his spine. Any time he left a john, Marco always suffered a frantic moment when he'd slap his pockets, or dig into them, hoping he had not forgotten to take the money, or lost it, or had it picked out from his pockets. He always found it. And the john had always paid him the right amount. But when he saved money, he hid it somewhere for later, then had trouble finding it again.

As he sorted out the history of caching the money he had saved, Marco opened the junk drawer. The envelope was there. He had written the date on the outside when he sealed the envelope, but the envelope was open, the top edge cut, as if with a knife. The two thousand dollars he had managed to save, and the money clip with which it was held together, were gone. He rummaged through the drawer because he had the vague memory of having added to his money, or having taken some out, and having used a clean envelope for the new amount. Then he remembered moving that envelope from the drawer to another part of the room, into one of the small drawers of the vanity perhaps, or under the mattress, or some other place he was desperate to remember.

The money was not in any of the other places.

He told himself to remember where he had moved it so that he wouldn't freak out, but he was freaking out. He dumped the contents of the drawer on the floor. The money had to be there. He just had to look again.

It was there. It had to be there.

That was the part that killed him.

He knew it was there. He just couldn't find it.

summer

fifteen

The sky was gray and burdened with clouds and the trees trapped in the rear courtyard swayed in the gusts. Marco heard the wind howl and figured, because of the chill in his room, that it was cold today. Outside, the wind blew warm and rank, and as Marco headed up the street to the subway, the sweater he'd put on at home was making him sweat. He didn't think about taking it off. He pressed forward, entrenched in a routine that he questioned as little as he did the alarm clock that yanked him awake every morning. He got up, never understanding why, or for what, and moved with the pace of the others.

The heat on the subway platform was unbearable. A muggy wind stirred when the trains heaved in and out of the station. Everyone had dark spots dampening their armpits or collars. The men carried their suit jackets folded over their arms, but the sweat still poured out of them, at the forehead, or at the back of the neck. Marco felt his own perspiration beading between his legs, and tried to ignore the faint stink assaulting his nose. Everyone smelled, as if backed up and stagnant, in need of draining.

Marco had trouble breathing inside the train cars. A few windows were open, but whatever air came though was knotted with fumes and coupled with the screech of the wheels against the tracks. The lights flickered, threatening to go out, and the wheels sent sparks of light though the tunnel, illuminating the graffiti tagged on the dark stretches between stations.

When he got to work, one of the high school girls was already there. They came more often now that school was out for the summer. The office was crowded, but there was still little to do. Mr. Ehrenkratz either didn't know about it or didn't care. He might have kept everyone on the payroll out of pity. The crush of bodies and the ceaseless run of mouths, like a talk show in which no one shut up about themselves, left Marco with sharp headaches. Today was supposedly the longest day of the year, a terrible little fact the high school girl was telling her friend on the phone. These days, Marco thought to himself, had too many hours.

He sat at his desk, running his hand across the back of his head, feeling the sharp stubble of a recent haircut. He felt lulled by the touch of his hair, undisturbed by everyone coming in late, complaining about the heat and the packed trains. Che bitched about her roommate.

"I'll smoke a cigarette on the can when I'm constipated," she said. "I learned that in England. Smoking there wasn't such a desperate thing as it is here. But Ali pukes his lungs out every morning. He doesn't calm down until he gets that first long drag. In London, everyone's much more cool about it."

She lived there one semester through a college exchange program, but she talked about it the way most people talked about their hometowns, and everyone in New York seemed to be from somewhere else. Towns that did not even warrant a spot of ink on a map.

England was the last place Marco wanted to hear about. For all he knew, that was where Chris had run off with his money. He was sure of it since the money never surfaced. Chris had to have taken it.

It could have been no one else. Sol never went into his room. That was what she claimed. The apartment had not been broken into. The windows were intact, the grates locked, the door bolted. No one could have come in from outside to take the money. No one would have found it in his junk drawer.

Marco had called Hotel Seventeen to see if Chris had left a forwarding address or phone number, but the number he got for him turned out to be his own. He kept going over the facts in his head, the number of months he had saved, the nights, the men, the way it all added up to nothing. At first he didn't want to think Chris had taken the money, but he started to believe it when he called his answering service a few days later and picked up a message from Quentin. Then it made sense. The payback Chris had been nagging him about. He never thought Chris was serious about taking a percentage of what he made from Quentin. It wasn't his fault Quentin wanted him.

England, Marco mumbled to himself as he sat at his desk. He had nothing to do but think. Richard, the john Chris had left bankrupt, lived somewhere in England. He had always wanted Chris to move there with him. Marco hated everything about Richard, his round, liver-spotted forehead, the wispy white laurel around his ears, the teeth that seemed rotted from tobacco. He wore gold-framed glasses, which he probably called spectacles.

Fiona, a new hire from Barnard, came into the office later that morning, complaining about the accompanist in her dance class.

"He's so frightening," Che agreed. She had taken the same class. "He's like a dirty old man."

"Worse," Fiona said, standing in the middle of the office, all faces on her like stage lights. "He gave me this, like, little crumpled piece of paper that asked if I want to go out with him or something and I'm like, yeah, right. I'd never go out with you. No way. And then when I go back to my room to get ready to come down here, my roommate hands me this other note and says, you're never going to believe what happened this morning before anatomy class. Some old guy came up and gave me this note. That note was like, hey, let's get together and do something some night."

"No!" Che squealed.

"Yes. It was him. I knew it was him. It was like the same kind of paper and the writing was all weird and scraggly. So I took the notes, both of them, and went back to dance class and told Professor Turner about it."

"Oh, I remember her. She's nice. What did she say?"

Fiona narrowed her eyes and looked around the room. "She said it would be taken care of." She burst out laughing, but no one else laughed with her. "You think he's going to get fired?"

"He better," Che huffed.

"Yeah, he should, I guess. I mean there we are in the skimpiest clothes and he's watching us. It's not right."

"It's so not right."

"He was good, though." Fiona sighed. "Did he ever play the violin for you guys? It was so beautiful."

"Oh, he was brilliant."

"There's more," Fiona said. "Zoe, my marvelously stupid friend, went to a concert at Carnegie Hall with him."

"Zoe the blond?" Che asked. She seemed to know everyone.

Fiona nodded and a smile broke across her face.

"She is so stupid. It's that modern dance thing. They are so not there. I mean, how could she have gone out with him in the first place and then admit it? Scary."

Fiona giggled and put her bag away under her desk and then fled to the bathroom. The entire front office went quiet again, as if Fiona had never arrived or as if the curtains had closed on her first act. Marco didn't want to hear about dirty old men. They reminded him too much of the theater and his appointment with Jean later that night. He didn't need the money. At least, he wasn't broke. But he wanted to have a nice dinner. It had been a while since anyone had taken him to dinner. He doubted he would have had the patience for anyone other than Jean, but who knew, he might still have gone out with someone else. He felt he belonged to the men because they wanted him. At the office, where he felt separated from the girls, as if their desks lay across an ocean, he never knew who he was. He blamed some of the alienation on the fact that his work, when he had any to do, changed from day to

174

day. One day he typed letters, on another he delivered orders of names to cold-calling stockbrokers who would nearly mob him when he arrived with the leads, and other days he just rearranged his desk, the horoscopes pasted to his computer, and filed the lunch menus of the nearby restaurants and takeout joints.

This week, his job was to check the names that had been sent back from the stockbrokers for incorrect phone numbers. Lou wanted him to call up every tenth name out of the two thousand. Marco called, as he was told, and asked for Susan or Roberta, Larry or Eugene, in places like Boring, Oregon, and Destin, Florida. When he came upon cities in Pennsylvania, places like Punxsutawney and Luciusboro, Haycock and Defiance, he wondered how far they were from Erie, where Jaime had grown up. Marco kept getting the urge to call him and ask where exactly Lovejoy, another city that snared his attention, stood in relation to Erie, but that thick rope of desire which had once braided Jaime and him together now seemed as limp as a string between tin cans. Nothing passed between them except the hollow beat of time.

When Fiona got back from the bathroom, she had a call waiting from the university police who wanted her to return to school to identify the man who had given her the note.

For lunch, Marco went to a small shop that sold flavored coffees and sandwiches made with bread of every known grain. The food was expensive, but since he didn't want to eat too much before his dinner with Jean, he only ordered a cup of soup.

The women on the stools all clutched their black leather handbags as they ate their mixed green salads. When they stood up and shook themselves like pigeons in a birdbath, Marco knew it was time for him to head back. He was easily missed, since only he went out for lunch. Everyone else at the office ordered in: Che because she said once she went into work, she didn't want to go out again, and Irene because she hated to eat alone and didn't want people to think she didn't have friends.

Marco had almost stopped going out himself. He had been at a corner deli last week, poking around the hot and cold food bar, trying to decide what to eat, when a middle-aged man came up to him and asked if he still danced. Marco tried to place him, but couldn't. "You're Marco, right," the man had whispered. Marco nodded, putting back his empty plastic container, his appetite dropping out of his stomach. The man said he had a place around the corner. It would take only ten minutes. Fifteen at most. Marco told him he had retired and rushed back to the office.

Today, he wasn't ready to return to work so fast. Most of the numbers he was cold-calling were disconnects with no forwarding numbers. Some had moved. Others were dead; had been for several years, the people on the other end shrieked before slamming their phones down. Some hung up as soon as he asked to speak to the person on his list.

His neck hurt from cradling the phone against his shoulder all morning. He didn't have the stamina to drag himself back to work, pretend to do his job, and listen to the girls. He thought of staying at the café and buying himself some dessert: tiramisu or rice pudding or a piece of the chocolate cake in the display case. He didn't even like chocolate, but he would have bought it to see if it made him feel any better. The girls at the office seemed to forget themselves after a bit of chocolate. That's what they said. Of course, they talked about a lot of things. They talked about the same problem boyfriends and department store sales, much like the radio station that played the same five songs all day, but no one listened to each other. He would have done anything to keep from returning to work, even step into the deadly path of a delivery boy speeding down the sidewalks on his bicycle.

The warm wind pushing him, a crumpled brown bag of grief, Marco approached the office building. He could almost hear Che ranting at the copy machine and Irene talking into the phone while eating Chinese take-out, their words mixing with the sharp smell of scallions and broccoli. At the glass doors leading into the lobby he turned away.

He stopped at the New David porn theater. It was closed, a metal grate shuttered over the entrance, and underneath the metal links an orange notice blazed. A Department of Health violation. Across the street, he noticed the peep booths were open, the neon promise of buddy booths flashing with possibility. He decided against it. It was too early for sex, and he also didn't want anyone from the office seeing him. And who knew? He might find one of their own sweaty salesmen in a booth. The thought disgusted him and he continued down the street. The guys working the sidewalks shouted at him to check out this or that strip joint and practically shoved complimentary passes into his ass. He flung the invites into the street without stopping.

On Broadway, a building advertised retail space available. The signs posted above the street-level tenants promised renters and buyers: YOU WILL BE IN THE CENTER OF THE ENTERTAINMENT WORLD, YOU WILL BE IN THE CENTER OF THE FINANCIAL WORLD, YOUR BUSINESS WILL BE PROMOTED DISCREETLY OR BOLDLY. The signs reminded him of selling sex for money. He figured he was discreet since he never mentioned it to anyone. Not to anyone at the office. The thrill of being wanted, at least by strangers, had flickered out a long time ago. Who would have thought?

Going through Times Square, Marco felt unfazed by the lights, unimpressed and unmoved by the crowds on the sidewalks, the daredevils who darted across the intersection in the face of snarling yellow cabs. He turned without having any clear destination and came to the theater. The hand-lettered sign listed the dancers for the week. He found himself climbing the steps, as if he had been planning to come here all along. The world suddenly seemed to right itself when he got to the box office and saw Esther behind the glass. He wasn't going back to his desk job now. Not even to say he quit. His body felt strong as he stood at the top of the stairs, solid, present. His bad knee didn't even hurt.

Two muscle guys slid out the door and bounded down the stairs together. Marco didn't recognize them and they didn't look at him. Esther, sitting behind the glass, reading a magazine, didn't seem to notice him either. He tapped the glass and smiled and told Esther he just wanted to look at the show for a few minutes. She said he had to pay the full price. He reminded her that he danced there. She said she knew. She remembered him, but if he wanted to come in, he was going to have to pay the full price—something about the new theater policy.

He expected the regular crowd and then he remembered this was a weekday afternoon. He had only worked weekends. He never tried to want anything that two nights at the theater couldn't buy. He didn't want the wholesale life Chris had led, doing three or four shows a day during the week, then the marathons on weekends. Marco didn't have that kind of endurance, not so much for the dancing, but for the men.

Marco sat in the audience and leaned back in his seat and noticed the theater wasn't as dark as he remembered. The red bulbs had been replaced with cool blue ones, and there were more of them. A beefy man in a T-shirt with the word "GUARD" slapped across his swollen chest, walked the perimeter of the seats, occasionally shining his flashlight into the dimness where a few men sat upright and still. Despite the smiling naked dancer on stage, Marco felt uneasy, as if he was struggling through a porn movie while his parents sat next to him. He tried to shrug it off, focusing on the dancer who must have been the one advertised that week as the body beautiful. His body was especially grotesque with its swells and rips of muscle. He wore a pair of gym pants with a reflective running stripe along the leg and a floppy black hat that was popular with rebels in Central America and roughneck street kids. The next dancer wore a cap too. His name was Joey and he strutted to an awful song that kept repeating the mundane words "Jersey City Noise." Pierre wore a baseball cap and only removed it at the end of his set, as if seeing the top of his head was as significant as seeing his dick.

Sometime in the middle of the show, the DJ's voice failed to register. It wasn't Manuel, but whomever it was called out the dancers in the same weathered whisper. The DJ introduced the next performer and added that the audience would really enjoy him. The dancer was just another muscled mass sauntering around the stage. He couldn't dance. He ran his fingers through his greasy curled hair and then over his body. He peeled off his tank top and then unbuttoned his jeans. The few pubes he hadn't shaved or plucked were already showing and Marco realized that none of the dancers wore underwear anymore. He didn't understand. His entire time at the theater, underwear was as important, if not more, than showing dick. Everyone had their particular taste. The boys from the outer boroughs usually wore bright-colored bikinis, the kind that came three to a package. Others wore Calvin Klein or whatever brand happened to be advertised on the huge billboards towering over Times Square. Marco wore plain white briefs. The men he went out with liked them. Nothing out of the ordinary, but erotic, they would say. Briefs were what his mother bought him when he was a kid.

A hairy Italian named Mario came out next. His nose belonged on a statue, sharp and perfect, but the rest of him wasn't so wonderful. He couldn't dance either. He kept looking up at the lights, reaching for them, stretching his torso up so that the muscles would show. During the second number, when the guy was naked and spreading his hairy ass, Marco retreated to the lounge. He grabbed a few pretzels and sat down. One of the first dancers nodded to him. It was an aside that meant nothing. The dancer went off and Marco remained sitting, wondering if any of the other dancers were going to approach him, or if any of the johns would. One in particular, a john with stubble like cactus spikes, kept passing Marco. He glanced at Marco now and then, but never came up to him. Marco promised himself that he would leave in a few minutes.

The lamp light struggled to keep the shadows from spreading like bruises. Marco stood, most of his clothes still on, his fly open. The john sucked and the sucking felt good. Marco liked this: He could be sitting at the theater, and then find himself in a hotel room, or an apartment overlooking the Hudson River, as he was now.

The john slowly rose off his knees, lifting Marco's shirt to kiss his stomach and ribs and nipples, and as he kissed him around the neck, Marco caught the stench of the john's mouth. The john tried to kiss Marco on the lips, but Marco moved his face away. The john kept going, nibbling Marco's ears, then sweeping a smelly tongue across Marco's jaw. Marco pulled back, sickened by the wetness, and the john looked hurt.

Marco pecked the john's cheek as consolation, but the skin felt bumpy, as if from razor burn. The john stepped back to look at Marco, to stare into his eyes, collect all the romantic illusions he'd paid for. Marco couldn't take his eyes off the john's cheeks, which were covered with pimples no bigger than the head of a pin, sharp and red, as if dabbed with a crimson ink. They glistened in the feeble light.

"What's the matter?" the john asked.

"I don't know," Marco said, meaning he didn't know what pickled the john's face. He hadn't noticed it at the theater.

The john's voice broke. "Are you sure?"

Marco started zipping his pants. "I should go."

"Please don't do that," the john said, grabbing Marco's crotch.

"I'm sorry. I can't do this. I can't."

"What's the matter?"

"Nothing," Marco snapped and buckled his belt. "I just can't do this."

"Is this your first time?" The john reached for Marco again.

Marco didn't answer. He let the john hold him so that he'd be satisfied and let him leave. He felt he owed him that much.

"I'm sorry," Marco said, breaking the stillness and pacing the room as if in search of the clothes he never took off. The john reached for him, but Marco jerked away. "I gotta go."

"Don't be sorry," the john said. "This is actually good news. You're too nice a person to be doing this sort of thing. You can get a real job. It's not hard. You can get a real job and a real life, and who knows?" The john's voice went flat. He lit a cigarette and sat on his bed. "I'm happy for you. Sad for me because this always happens. The last kid I fell for worked out of a hotel bar in Boston. Sweet kid. And young. I guess he was twenty, twenty-one. I helped him get out of the business. Then he found a boyfriend and I never saw him again."

Marco nodded. Great story, he thought to himself. He gave the john a pitying smile and walked toward the door.

"You don't have to leave now," the john choked. He beat his chest to ease the smoke trapped in his lungs. "Do you have to leave now?"

"I should."

"You don't have to."

"I want to," Marco said with hard beats on each word.

"Fine," the john offered. He stubbed his cigarette into an ash-tray and grabbed a pair of pants lying on the floor. He pulled out his card and a few bills. "Here," he said, holding them out to Marco. "Take this and promise to call me."

"Sure," Marco said, stuffing the wad into his jeans.

He hurried out into the warm streets, the thick air hanging like the damp sheets of a ruined night. He walked a few blocks before he pulled the money out of his pocket. Already the bills felt thin in his hands. There weren't enough of them. He counted two singles, a five, a ten. He tore up the john's card and gave the ten to a man begging on the street. The man ran after him, shouting to everyone along the way that this guy, this guy he was pointing to, had given him a ten-dollar bill. Ten dollars. Ten! The beggar kept shouting, asking Marco his name. Marco turned around and told him if he didn't shut up he was going to take the ten back. The man ran off without another word.

Marco kept the other seven dollars and went into a café on Greenwich Avenue where the raw floorboards creaked. An espresso machine hissed in the rear and a few strains of classical music played overhead. Despite the one or two couples, the place felt empty, sad almost, because hardly anyone spoke, and there were too many abandoned tables and wire-backed chairs twisted into silent hearts. A short old woman with legs swollen into stumps came to ask his order.

"What'll you have?" she asked.

"Coffee and whatever you have for dessert."

"We got apple crumb pie with whipped cream."

Marco nodded. The words "whipped cream" failed to register until she returned to the table with the pie and its white mound. The sight of it made him groan.

"Can I have it without the cream?" he asked, pushing the pie back.

"How can you have it without cream?" She looked at him blankly. "It's no good without it. I always serve it like this. Have been for twenty-five years. Probably more years than you got on you."

"Fine," Marco grumbled and began to stab through the cream to get to the pie. He took a bite and watched the old woman shove off to the back. In her wake, a strange familiarity lapped against him. He found himself, nineteen and sitting in a diner, eating a slice of pie, hungry for a passing glance from anyone who might want him. He had always been waiting. Like a continent to be conquered, Chris used to joke. Chris wanted to be the lone missionary sent to settle and stake claims. It was easier, Marco knew, to get taken than to search for what you truly wanted. The seeker risked a broken heart. Marco hadn't picked Chris. Chris had picked him, as the johns would later, as everyone had in his life. He let them come to him. He risked nothing more than a sexually transmitted disease.

Jaime had been the only one with whom he had risked anything. But what had he risked? What had he ventured? An invitation to a crummy hotel? A few dinners? He'd chosen Jaime, and Jaime seemed to have chosen him. It was the biggest leap in Marco's life, crossing that fear like a man who had dreamed of swimming over to *el otro lado*. Now he had to keep moving. He'd been resting on the muddy banks congratulating himself, when really, it was the same dingy borderlands on either side. He had to go further, deep into where the dream lay, the dream he hadn't even dreamt yet.

Marco's tired eyes darted to various faces and he listened to every scrape of sound. He hadn't risked enough, or made clear to Jaime that he wanted him. He didn't want the other men. He didn't want to kiss another anonymous mouth. He didn't want to get sucked by someone he didn't care for. And he was tired of waiting. He took a final stab at the pie, pushed his chair back, and left some money before going outside to find a pay phone.

As he neared Jaime's street, Marco thought he'd stumbled onto a movie set. A squad of police cars was parked on the sidewalk and rows of barriers blocked the street. A battery of lights cut across the face of the buildings. The zigzag fire escapes looked like rusting stitches.

"You live on this street?" a cop asked Marco as he tried to pass.

"I'm going to see a friend," Marco said, not bothering to stop, but the cop grabbed him by the arm.

"Where?" he hissed.

"I said I was going to see a friend?"

"Building number, smart-mouth."

"I don't know," Marco said, trying to free himself.

"So how do you know where you're going?"

"I've been there before."

The cop shoved him back roughly. "Call them on the phone," he said. "Tell them they have to come get you at the gate." He turned to look at the other cops sitting in their patrol cars. They laughed to themselves.

"I don't have a quarter," Marco said.

"Too bad," the cop said and laughed.

A couple of kids rode their bikes through a gap in the barricade and the cop shouted at them to get off. Marco tried to slip through then, taking a few steps, but the cop's hand clamped down on his shoulder.

"Punk, don't make me hurt you." He dragged Marco to the edge of the street. "I told you, only residents and their guests. Don't you understand? Speak English? Now get out or I'll have you arrested."

Marco shot him the finger and ran off to find a pay phone. He called Jaime again and told him what had happened. Jaime laughed and said he'd forgotten to warn him. The city had just gutted the squats across the street from him and had thrown everyone in jail. The cops were there to keep the peace. Jaime said he would meet Marco at an Italian restaurant down the block. Marco agreed, not mentioning that he wasn't hungry or that he only had a few bucks.

It started to rain. Marco waited in front of the restaurant despite it. He didn't mind getting wet. It was a relief from the heat that had hung in the air most of the day. He watched people struggling with their broken umbrellas, the black nylon flapping like a bird's lamed wing. Jaime came down the sidewalk with a huge umbrella and an arrogant stride that seemed to know he could walk anywhere, even back into Marco's life, if he chose to.

Marco was too nervous to say anything. He didn't kiss Jaime or shake his hand or pat him on the back. He only followed him into the restaurant. As they waited for a table, their eyes kept meeting, but Jaime seemed elsewhere, either from hunger or from the drinking he'd confessed to earlier on the phone. He'd been at it since lunch time. Marco wanted to think Jaime's glance meant something, communicated a hard to admit attraction, but then he caught him noticing a pale, short-haired guy at a rear table. The guy stared back in their direction, looking at Jaime.

The hostess sat them at a table next to the stranger, and for the next few minutes, Marco watched Jaime's eyes wander to the guy. Jaime was either too drunk to notice what he was doing or didn't care. Everyone else in the restaurant seemed to go on about everything, yapping away like dogs at the dog run, their owners elsewhere, perhaps talking to other owners. Marco felt diminished by the conversations. The restaurant windows were open to the street and out there even the cabs seemed capable of sustaining their own speech, the bald tires hissing, brakes grinding, horns blowing, and their flashing signal lights keeping a whole other specialized language. Marco looked at the clocks on the walls, those stacked in the recessed shelves, and those suspended from the ceiling. They all had different times, but none of them seemed right.

"How long has it been?" Marco asked.

"Don't worry. The food's coming."

"I mean how long have we been 'hanging out?' Your term, not mine."

"I thought you liked that," he said, clumsily folding his arms.

"Hanging out doesn't mean much to me. So? How long?"

"Five months. Maybe six."

"That long?" Marco knew it was longer. "Isn't five months long?"

"Depends on what you want." His smile threatened to swallow his face.

"I want a boyfriend."

"A boyfriend? You make it sound like high school."

The way Jaime bunched his face in a sneer was the most animated thing he had done that night. It wasn't the reaction Marco wanted. Still, he pressed forward, pushing himself as he had most of that day. The longest day he could remember. He smoothed the napkin on his lap and tried again to say what he needed to say.

"I just want a little security," he said. "I need to know whether you still want to see me or not. I hate having that doubt."

"I don't know," Jaime said. "I just take it day by day, nothing too far into the future."

Marco looked down at his napkin. He kept unfolding and refolding it until it resembled a battered war flag of surrender. He turned back to Jaime and smiled, the exertion straining a nerve in his cheek, causing it to jerk without his wanting it to.

"How's work?" Marco asked, though he didn't want to ask about work. "Have you been to the theater?"

"I haven't been there in a while. A couple guys got busted last time I was there."

"Undercover cops?"

"I don't know. They just never came back for the next show."

Marco nodded. "You ever think of quitting?"

"Do you?" Jaime brought his face over the table, his eyes wide and sloppy with alcohol. He glared at Marco for a dull moment. "I know you haven't quit. I know you still see them but you don't tell me. You play yourself off as some redeemed altar boy." He pulled himself back to his chair. "Why is it such a secret now? I'm still working. I'm not afraid to admit it. But you let this come between us. You won't have sex with me. It's like I'm dirty or something."

"You always want to have sex," Marco said in hushed tones, not wanting the guy at the next table to hear them. "It's never anything but sex."

"Well, sex is what I do best." He laughed. "It's my job."

"I don't want to be a job."

"You're not."

Marco looked up across the room, as if the hands of the clocks might point him to what he should say next, how to explain the feelings that ticked in him. "I want us to be different from all that. Do you know what I'm saying? It should be more than just sex."

Jaime didn't say anything. He had turned to look at the guy at the next table.

Marco tapped his water glass. "Can you at least look at me?"

"I think I know him."

"You've looked at every guy in here. Why don't you just ask them all?" Marco turned to the stranger next to them. "Excuse me, but do you know my friend here?" Marco wondered why he had not said "boyfriend," but still, the guy shook his head no. Marco turned to Jaime. "There. He doesn't know you. Now can you stop cruising the restaurant?"

"I wasn't cruising," he said behind an attenuated smile. "I thought I knew him."

"Well, he doesn't know you. Listen to me." Marco reached for Jaime's hands but Jaime pulled them away and dropped them under the table. "We have to talk about where we're going."

"Look, I don't know how to tell you this, but I know nothing about the Philippines. I've never been there."

"I'm not talking about the Philippines." Marco tried to find Jaime's hands under the table but Jaime's leg was crossed and he only came across the wet heel of Jaime's shoe. He wiped his hand against the tattered napkin. "I'm talking about us. It makes me crazy just thinking you'll meet another guy."

"I haven't."

"You make it sound like you've been looking."

Jaime glanced again at the guy at the next table, but then his eyes settled back on Marco. He sipped his water and swallowed hard, his nostrils flaring. "Okay," he said. "I've slept with other guys. There. That's proof. The test that my feelings for you haven't changed."

"Well the test obviously failed." Marco threw his napkin on the table. "If you had feelings for me at all, you wouldn't have slept with anyone. I haven't been with anyone because you're the only one I want to be with. I love you."

Jaime nodded.

The nod reminded Marco of all the times the johns had confessed their love for him. He nodded, too, or thanked them, acknowledging how they felt and then forgot about it. At first, he did it only because he didn't know how else to deal with it. Then he continued to do it because there was no other way. He accepted the fact that they loved him, or said they did, and he said nothing to encourage or discourage it. They felt the way they did. He had done his job. A simple nod and nothing else was needed of him. The johns never pushed for more than that. They were too afraid of rejection.

Marco looked at Jaime a moment, at the way the light gleamed against the fall of his hair, and then excused himself, feeling perhaps what the johns felt, an impossible pain in the stomach, like being drop-kicked by an East Village street punk. Marco struggled to his feet and tried to navigate between the crowded tables. Every face turned to him, without bothering to see him, their mouths still going with words or food. A waitress directed him to the bathroom, pointing it out to him as if he had already shit in his pants.

He stumbled through the dimness and reached the bathroom. The door was locked. He banged to no response. He paced the little hall and watched the light seeping out from under the door. He would have banged again to get the constipated bastard out of there, or the heroin addict, or the sex fiend, whoever they were, but his pathetic drill would have been no improvement over theirs. What would he have done locked in the bathroom? Looked at himself in the mirror? Repeated to himself, I love you, Jaime, I love you. He had said that. He'd actually said he loved him, and all Jaime had done was nod back. Nod. Which wasn't even a thank you. The least Jaime could have done, Marco thought, was twitch or pretend to swat the words away like venomous little flies that had escaped his mouth. Chris would have thrown a ticker tape parade or called *The New York Times* to run the headline: MARCO SAYS I LOVE YOU.

Marco laughed to himself, imagining the announcement flashing on the electronic strip sign at the hustler bar, or sliding across the zipper over Times Square. It was news. Marco had finally proved Chris wrong. He wasn't cold. He wasn't insular. He could love. He was capable of feeling and able to express it. The thing was, he hadn't expected his heart to empty out and burn down like a church on fire.

He lifted his fist to bang on the bathroom door again, but he let it go and turned back toward the dining room. He watched Jaime from the distance. The beauty mark below his nose seemed like a final punctuation to what Marco had thought they could have together. The next table over had emptied, so Jaime sat alone, drinking a glass of wine he must have ordered. The waitress brought out their food, large bowls of pasta topped with basil and garlic. Marco thought he could smell it from where he stood. He took a final look at Jaime, and without waiting to see if his eyes might flash and notice him, or whether he might start eating without him, Marco mouthed out, like a *pendejo*, he knew, but he had to, "I Love You." Then he hurried out of the restaurant.

He went up the block in sharp strides, as if forced by a mechanism unwinding in his gut. He did not notice the rain or the cops at their barricades. The world was a blur as he walked, and he cried as he went.

It was half past four the next morning when Marco sat at the Key West Diner on Broadway. He hated the obnoxious colors, but he'd been walking the city all night. From the Italian restaurant, he'd escaped to Tompkins Square Park, and roamed through the dark before realizing that he was too close to Jaime's apartment. He walked to Hotel Seventeen and lingered on the front steps a moment before heading to Stuyvesant Park. Approaching the entrance, imagining Chris had used the same gates, he noticed the sign that named the park Stuyvesant Square. He'd called it by the wrong name all this time. It was still a cruising spot, though, as far as he could tell, watching the guys ride around on bikes. Others walked dogs. A couple of women sat together on a bench and a homeless guy had stationed himself with his cart in a distant corner where the lights were shot out. Marco sat near the fountain and watched the furtive parade of guys. He kept telling himself he would get up and follow the next guy who looked in his direction. He waited and the waiting forced him to see that going with any of the guys would have been too easy. And an easy life, a fortune cookie once claimed, taught nothing. Marco wanted to think it was the fortune cookie Jaime had left at the noodle shop where they first shared a meal, but he wasn't sure. Every cookie came with forgettable folk wisdom. The slips of paper may as well have been left blank for your own debatable genius.

From where he sat, the Con Ed tower was visible, its colored lights stark against the violet night sky, but he couldn't see the face of the clock. He remained there too long, then wandered up Broadway, to Times Square. The city had knocked off to sleep. The signs had winked out, the huge television hung black and mute. He took his time as he walked, reading the graffiti on the shuttered grates, waving to the homeless men who waved to him from inside the temporary residences of ATM booths. When Marco reached his street in the early hours, he refused to go home, and went to the Key West instead, where he slumped now.

He sat at the counter, accompanying the Mexican guy cleaning the silverware and talking about his old life in Aguas Calientes. Marco nodded now and again, sipping at his coffee, trying not to fall under the hypnotic glare of the plastic-wrapped donuts. He snapped awake whenever the Mexican said one particular Spanish word or phrase that reminded him of where he came from, of his parents, of who he once was. For so long, he had no choice but to believe what everyone said about him, like his father, who claimed Marco belonged to him, and owed him in so many ways. Marco wanted to belong to himself. Be on his own.

Marco stared down at his coffee and laughed to himself. He'd escaped his father only to get caught by Chris, and by other men who began to cart off pieces of him like a quarry that would never run out of whatever it was they wanted.

A man beside Marco asked him what was funny. Marco turned and looked at him. He hadn't noticed him there before and couldn't imagine how he'd missed him. He was middle-aged, like any one of his johns, but this man at the counter was in a pair of cut-off shorts and had a small dog yapping at his feet. There was a law against having a dog inside a diner. Marco knew that and wished the Mexican would throw them out, but the Mexican was probably undocumented, illegal, afraid of any attention he might draw to himself. Wouldn't want to get deported back to Aguas.

"Share the joke," the man insisted and the dog yelped beside him.

Marco shook his head to dismiss it, not wanting to get into a conversation, but the man pressed, or rather the dog did. It padded over and sniffed Marco's tired feet.

"I think he likes you," the man said.

Marco groaned to himself. He thought it cruel and pathetic to use the dog. The man probably had it for no other reason than to snare strangers in the park or on the street.

"He must know you somehow," the man said.

Marco asked the Mexican for a refill and tried to ignore the dog as best he could, but it was difficult because the dog kept running around under Marco's legs and tried to jump on his lap a few times. Marco eventually reached down and petted the thing. It wasn't the dog's fault.

"You a student?" the man asked, coming another stool closer.

"No," Marco replied, reminded of how Chris used to tell the johns he was putting himself through school, which was true, but clichéd. Maybe the man knew Chris and was now forever asking everyone if they were students too.

"Are you an artist?" the man asked.

"No," Marco replied. He looked at the waiter and smirked.

"A musician?"

"No."

"Oh," the man said, but still no tone of defeat. "Are you a dancer?"

For a moment, Marco thought the man might have recognized him from the theater, but there was no way, since he hadn't danced in months. He wanted to say no again, that he was nothing, nobody, but the nights he partnered his mother at the various dances came waltzing back. Those nights had excited him once.

His mother would buy him new clothes because she wanted him to look good when she presented him. *"Mira, este es m'hijo,"* she would say, getting the attention of entire tables. *Conocidos,* she called them, and would push him forward so that the admiring men and women would give him a pat so that he would not wake the following morning sick from *mal ojo.* His mother was always suffering from it, the feverish and debilitating mystery that struck whenever she went out dancing, which she said came not so much from an evil stare than from a desirous one. Marco's father found it amusing, joking that it was the fattest women, *las más gorditas*, who seemed to contract the superstitious ailment most. He said it was nothing but a hangover.

When his mother seemed satisfied with the introductions and bored by the ensuing small talk, she would pull Marco to the dance floor to turn and roll in the revolving circle of couples. They danced for hours, each song a variation of familiar tragedies and loss, melancholic melodies to which they two-stepped and turned. Marco liked the Cotton-Eyed Joe in which everyone held onto one another by the shoulder and kicked their heels and shouted obscenities. He liked the Bunny Hop as well, even in his teens, because then he could hold the waist of some cute guy, the music going faster until all the bodies smashed against each other in one writhing line.

It was in the bathrooms of whatever place they were—the local veteran's hall, community center, or low-ceilinged ballroom—where Marco first felt the wrenching tug of desire. Standing at the porcelain troughs that served as urinals, a chill air rising from the ice cubes which acted as a kind of splash guard, a few of the older men would leer at him as they pulled on their dicks, flashing him before zipping up.

In New York, Marco went to a few dance studios and took classes in jazz funk and hip-hop, the kind of popular street moves that blurred across music videos. He was never as good as the aspiring professionals, but what amused him was that he was still making a living at it, but did not care enough about it to rehearse hour after hour, bandaging bloodied feet, to keep dancing. And, really, when he thought of it, it was not about dancing at all, but about what he did between the songs he danced to. What dance was he on now? What music played?

The man and his dog were gone and the Mexican had run to the washroom to get another rack of silverware. When he came back, drying and throwing the utensils into a compartment under the counter, Marco excused himself to the bathroom. It was all the coffee the Mexican had been pouring him, insisting he take another, like a long-lost *compadre* buying the drinks to celebrate his return. Marco obliged him. He didn't have the money to go anywhere else.

In the bathroom, he locked the door. He wanted to keep from looking at himself in the mirror, but he looked anyway, at his face, which was not as young as the johns liked to say. They probably only said it to help themselves along. Another illusion they needed to deceive themselves with, like thinking he could love them, or pretending to themselves that the money never mattered, or that they weren't actually cheating on their wives or lovers. Marco decided that his face was nothing more than that.

Without meaning to, he made a mess of himself, splashing his urine against the floor and on the tops of his shoes. He took them off to hold them under the dryer, then stopped. He sat on the toilet seat and dug a hand into the warm mouth of one shoe. He pulled out the tattered remains of Jaime's name, scraps he had rewritten only days ago, a doomed effort which had turned the fragile color of moths. He dropped the paper into the toilet and flushed.

He went back out to the counter in his socks. He figured if the Mexican had said nothing about the dog, he wouldn't say anything about not wearing shoes. No one else was in the diner anyway. Marco sat and sipped his fresh cup of coffee and felt lucky that the diner never closed. There was something about having seen its signs glowing in the dark, as if discovering the neon-hued walls for the first time, as if coming upon an island for which the diner was named. Key West had the southernmost reach in the United States. He had learned that in high school. It was the paradisiacal last stop before the drop into the ocean. The diner might not be the exotic escape Marco had intended, but it was a comfort this night, and he asked the Mexican for pencil and paper. The Mexican yanked a pencil from behind his ear and slapped down a scratch pad. He asked what he was doing, but Marco didn't answer, afraid it would slip and be lost forever.

The name was long and clumsy, a barbed fence of letters on which every tongue snagged. Teachers and students mispronounced it and he accepted the various nicknames he'd been given. He had never bothered to make anyone use his proper name once he left home. Chris had used it when they first started seeing one another. He liked to put in that extra roll of the tongue, but ever since moving to New York, he had settled on calling him Marco, as the johns did. Even Chris wasn't really named Chris. Marco had given him that name ever since Chris first confused him with the Marco of the personal ad. It was only fair. And appropriate. Chris used to joke that he had discovered Marco. Marco argued that he had always existed, long before Chris came to the diner in Houston like some misdirected Columbus.

Marco printed his own name, the one given to him at birth, but it came out at odd angles, like a tiny house of scrap wood and tin ready to fall in a heap. Reymundo. Work on it, he thought to himself. Fine. He'd practice later. The two pieces he had now written were good enough and he placed one in each shoe and tied the shoes to his feet. He checked the clock. A few minutes past six on a summer morning.

Outside, the buildings awoke with reluctant blinks of light in the windows, the bread and fruit and vegetable trucks made their deliveries, and the dry cleaners sputtered and muttered with steam. Reymundo took the city slowly, walking up the street, past the *bodegas* and bus stops where people already waited to get to their jobs, or home if they'd been working through the night. He took his pace with deliberate steps and made it to Central Park and to the reservoir. A few runners sprinted past in their shorts and T-shirts. He went up to the fence and poked his fingers through the chain-link. He breathed deep, taking the humid air that hung over the dark calm of the reservoir. The lampposts snapped off, one right after the other, as the sun shot over the East Side buildings. He filled his lungs again and let his arms fall limp to his side. He shook out his legs and walked the track, invoking his own name with each advancing step.

acknowledgments

I am indebted to my regular Thursday nights with Alex Gerber, Diane Hatz, and Corey Sabourin. The soy-milk smoothies and supportive criticisms were a great help. Thanks also to Jacqueline Woodson, who first read the manuscript, and encouraged me to dive deeper. Manuel Morales Mendez, one of my best readers and *un buen compadre* in literature, thanks so much for your letters over the years. Barry Joseph, Paul Murphy, and Ito Romo read the manuscript in its entirety and gave me their assessments with unexpected enthusiasm that pushed me to yet another revision.

A deep-felt thanks to Guillermo Castro, Regie Cabico, Brian Guanzon, Blaine Hopkins, Patrick DeMontbron, and Kam Lau for their friendship, some still intact, others not. Thanks to Alex Wein for giving me the time to go off and do my work without worry.

Thanks also to Jaime Manrique and Jaime Cortez for publishing excerpts of this novel. To Erin Clermont, *un beso* for stirring up new insights. Your sharp eye and invaluable notes helped hone this piece of work.

Besos y abrazotes fuertes for my family. Mom, Dad, and Marco, thanks for your unflagging love, even when my words left you desperate for breath. And, not to be forgotten, thank you, Diana Michelle Guerra.

about the author

Erasmo Guerra was born and raised in the Rio Grande Valley of South Texas. His work has been published in numerous journals and anthologies including *New Worlds: Young Latino Writers, Gay Travels: A Literary Companion, Bésame Mucho: New Gay Latino Fiction,* and *Virgins, Guerrillas, and Locas.* He is also the editor of the non-fiction collection *Latin Lovers: True Stories of Latin Men in Love.* He lives in New York City.